PUBLISHED BY GUTTER PRESS TORONTO

National Library of Canada Cataloguing in Publication

Berger, Tamara Faith
The way of the whore / Tamara Faith Berger.

ISBN 1-896356-57-5

I. Title.

PS8553.E6743W39 2004   C813'.6   C2004-902108-7

Editor: Emily Pohl-Weary
Designer: Kika Thorne

Gutter Press Publisher: Ed Sluga
Gutter Press Founder: Sam Hiyate

FIRST EDITION

PRINTED IN CANADA

THE WAY OF THE WHORE

THE WAY OF THE WHORE

TAMARA FAITH BERGER

GUTTER PRESS TORONTO

Sister, the Enchanter

has stolen my heart —

where can I go,

what can I do —

he took the breath from my lungs.

I'd gone to the river,

a jug on my head,

when a figure rose through the darkness.

Sister, it cast a sorcerer's noose

and it bound me.

What the world calls virtue suddenly

      vanished.

I performed a strange rite —

Mira may be a slave, sister,

but she herself

      chose whom to sleep with.

MIRABAI 1498-1550

I. MIRE

II. HALLUCINATION

III. VIGOUR

MIRE

Things are different in the middle of the night. Rooms, legs, eyes, whatever. The air's so full of static that no one can see, so everyone just acts, because all acts are fine.

The acts that have led me to the middle of the night always reveal their inevitable order. All my soft and black thoughts slide into a chain. Until at just the right moment, finally I'm lucid and I know how a cock can complete me. A good hard cock never leaves you alone.

But morning is broken on its way in. I don't care what anyone says.

꿈

"Men think a woman walking alone at night is a whore," said John. He was pulling off my underwear. "It doesn't even matter what she's wearing or how she's walking. If it's late on the streets and she's all by herself, he's gonna roll down his window and stare at her ass. It's like he's waiting for something Mira, that one tiny click when he knows that she's going to get in his car."

John had my underwear down at my feet. I kicked them off and twisted my legs together.

"No girl's going to get in a strange man's car," I said.

"You would."

"I would not."

John laughed as he worked at wrenching my thighs apart. "Yes you would, Mira."

"Stop. I would not!"

"You'd get in my car."

"No!"

"I'd follow you and keep telling you how hot your ass is."

"Shut up!"

"Oh yeah, I know you. You'd get in my car."

I rolled my eyes and kept struggling. It was like this every single time we saw each other.

"Come, Mira, come," John would end up crooning to my pussy. "Come baby come, please come, come, come…"

My mind wandered when he licked me. I scratched my arms and watched his bobbing head. His eyes were slit and heavy between my bent thighs. It didn't feel real. All I could feel was wetness on top of wetness.

I thought of how men always looked at me. How it happened this time when I was ten. I was at the supermarket with my father and the guy at the cash said: "You better keep a close watch on that one." His eyes squinted down at my chest when he said it, at the two lumps pressing up under my shirt. Then the guy made a noise, a grunt through closed lips. My father looked down at me and laughed quickly, too, but it sounded like he didn't really mean it.

When we got in the car, my father didn't say a word. He just turned up the news and started driving really fast. I put my forehead against the window and watched us pass all the cars. I could still feel that guy looking right through my shirt. For a second I thought my chest had pushed out more when he was staring at it. I heard my father's breathing get loud. Air scratched past the hairs of his moustache. Then something started happening. Between my thighs on the seat I felt hot little beats, like a pulse or a bird was whipping around down there. It started getting louder. I had to squeeze my thighs tight. I was trying not to make any sound from the pulsing, trying not to let it come out in my breaths.

When we finally got home, I kept hearing what the guy had said, how it made them both laugh. "You better keep a close watch on that one." I didn't really know what it meant. I thought the guy meant — maybe — I was pretty, but when I tried to think more about what he really meant, I felt strange. Lying on my bed, the pulsing wouldn't stop spreading. It filled up my underwear with hot little beats. It felt okay, it felt good, but I didn't want it to keep happening, because I thought my father knew what had happened. I thought, in the car, he could smell it.

Things started to happen more often after that. I would get that feeling around men, older men, men in stores and on the street. It was always when I thought I saw them looking at me, especially the ones I knew I'd never get to meet. The construction men working in crews on the road. The businessmen with their kids and their wives. The guys on the subway who sweat strange perfume. That beating between my legs started happening so much that I thought those men could see right through me. Just from the way I was standing or walking, I thought it meant I wanted them to see. All those beats inside my body, throbbing so loud.

Sometimes I'd imagine a man in my house, a stranger in the bathroom, watching me shower. His two big hands would open a towel when I stepped out. Then he'd dry me, rub me, move the towel really fast back and forth behind my shoulders, behind my back and all the way down. My flesh would shake close to the man's face. My ass red behind me, my eyes blooming wide. The strange man would follow me into my bedroom, his footsteps sounding in time to my beats. He'd stand over my bed while I pretended to sleep with one of my feet sticking out of the covers. Then one arm would fall out, an arm that lead to my chest. If I rolled on my side, the man would see more. He would see how my breasts were starting to grow from my body, how my nipples were getting hard, how my hair down there was thick. If I rolled on my back, the sheet would fall off and the man would see straight up between my legs. I'd spread them for him, I knew I would. I was pulsing so much there I'd have to. I thought that if the man could see me naked like that, just silently watching, then it would all be okay. I'd stay quiet while he touched me anywhere he wanted. I'd want him to come back every single night, too, so he could tell me how much bigger my breasts were getting. He could tell me how much more hair he was seeing on my vagina. How much more stuff he was feeling down there.

I'd never even really touched myself where I imagined a man doing it. Maybe if I had, then everything would've been different. "Mira, you're the sweetest," John always whispered after licking.

He pushed his chin up onto my stomach and wiped his glistening mouth with the sheet. I closed my soaking wet cunt. Maybe.

꙳

I met John when I was fifteen. I was working in this cafe on the weekends and he started coming in every Saturday, always waiting to order from me. He'd sit there drinking his coffee for at least an hour, looking out the window, then looking at me. One day, he came up to the counter when he finished his coffee.

"I have to tell you something," he said, leaning in. "You're a very pretty young woman, you know that?"

My face got hot. I stared down at my hands.

"What's your name?"

My lips were coming apart to speak, but my tongue wasn't there. John read the name tag pinned to my shirt.

"Mira? That's a beautiful name. Mira," he murmured. "Are you Spanish?"

I nodded.

"I'm John, by the way."

He reached out a hand but I couldn't lift my eyes from the counter. I was staring down at his weird rocky fist. It had little white scratches all over the knuckles.

"So, Mira, what do you like to do when you're not here?"

I couldn't believe it, this guy looked as old as my father! There was stubble around his lips and dark skin under his eyes. Didn't he know I was only fifteen? I was squeezing my hands together so hard they were going numb. A creeping smile hooked into my cheek. I felt John looking down at me, waiting for me to say something. I knew he must've known I was embarrassed.

"Well, it was really nice to meet you," John said quickly. "I'll see you again, Mira, okay?"

He walked so fast to the door it looked like he was limping. I didn't think he would look back at me from outside, but he did. He turned around and waved. There was this thick feeling under my chin, like his fingers were there. I was smiling again, that stupid smile that stuck on one side. I didn't like how he'd made me look. "Better keep a close watch on that one." I didn't like the way he looked, I knew that — his black chin, his thick hair, those scratches on his knuckles — but throughout my whole next week, I couldn't stop thinking about him. I knew that he was going to come in the next Saturday. I kept on hearing every small thing that he'd said to me: "You're a pretty young woman. You're a very pretty young woman, you know that?" No one had ever said anything like that to me before. It made that feeling beat up between my legs, this time more than I'd ever felt it. I had to cross my thighs and put my hands in between them to make it stop. I wanted it to stop because I thought it was going to make me do something with that guy when, I swear, I thought he was disgusting!

I told this girl at school what happened, because I didn't know what I should do when he came back. She said: "Go for it. Older guys know what they're doing." She said that an orgasm was a "muscle contraction" and that if you didn't have a "muscle contraction," you didn't have a real orgasm. She showed me her hand with all the fingers open and said, "like this, just like this." She was opening and shutting her fingers really quick.

I knew that that feeling had never happened to me.

John came back to my work the next Saturday. He came back the next week and the one after that. I started to be able to look at him a little more. We never said much after that first time, just the regular "hi, how are you?" and "fine, how are you?" which was okay, because I still did feel a bit creeped out that maybe he was coming in just because of me. He'd started giving me pretty big tips after buying his coffee, too. At least a dollar in coins, pressing them right into my palm. It always felt like he touched me too long when he did that. Maybe it was just me, though, and I was worrying about it for nothing.

Then, one Saturday, John came in to see me three times during my shift. Right before he left the last time, he leaned in really close. He smelled kind of weird, like my mother making meat.

He said: "Do you like Chinese food? Have you ever gone out with your friends for Chinese food? I know a really good restaurant near here."

I shrugged my shoulders. I couldn't really speak.

John touched my arm lightly. "I'll see you later, okay?"

That was the day he met me outside after I finished. It was still pretty warm out and he was sweating through his T-shirt. I could see the hairs on his chest stuck down in a line. He was shaking his head a bit, smiling at me. I was wearing a purple tank top and a purple skirt that came down to my knees. I wished that I was wearing something over my top.

John touched my arm again. This time he gave it a squeeze. "I bet you'd like something sweet to drink after work. You must be tired."

"No, it's okay," I said quickly.

We started walking down the street and I could feel my thighs rubbing together under my skirt. It made me want to sit down and cross my legs.

John went into a variety store and got me a ginger ale. He bought himself cigarettes. I started drinking too fast straight from the can and I got the hiccups. We both laughed at the high-pitched sounds that were coming out of me.

"I'm going to have to scare you, Mira!"

I couldn't believe I was walking down the street laughing with this guy. I couldn't believe that no one was really looking at us either. I didn't know if John knew I was only fifteen. But I didn't feel like doing anything to stop him when he put his arm all the way around me, or when his fingers started tickling my neck. He just kept joking that it was to scare me out of my hiccups.

We turned down a street I'd never been on. There were a few old-looking houses beside this huge apartment building with foil on the windows. I saw two kids waving down at us from a balcony. I was going to wave back, but John shifted my shoulders to turn us off that street. I felt like a car he was steering.

I didn't ask where we were going because John started asking me questions out of the blue, like: "Are your mother and father still married? Do you have a boyfriend?"

"Yes," I said, then, "No."

John was laughing at me. I kept swallowing instead of changing what I was saying.

"But you probably remember who told you about sex the first time, don't you?"

I shook my head.

John lit a cigarette and looked at me. We were walking pretty fast. "Listen," he said. "The first person who told me about sex was my uncle. He wasn't much older than me, six years or something, we were just kids, you know, but it pretty much scared the shit out of me. He said it like this: 'A man gets on a top of a woman and opens her up with his dick.' I swear that's what he said. I didn't know what he meant but I knew I wanted to, you know, who wouldn't? A man opens a woman up with his dick... I'd never even seen a woman naked, not even my mother, and my uncle just goes: 'Watch me. I'll show you.' I wasn't saying much back, so he started wrestling with me, the way we always did. I was on the floor, and I remember I was trying to look up at what he was doing but I couldn't really see, you know, I think he was holding his crotch through his pants. Then, he was kneeling between my legs and I heard him laughing, going, 'okay Johnny-John, you're the woman now,' and he started spreading my legs — really fucking wide. It felt weird, Mira. It felt all fucked up. I was just a kid who didn't know what was what. So the next thing I know he's pulling off his pants, they're down to his knees and his cock is out, you know, sticking straight out, and the only thing I could think was: man, that's big! What did I know? Fuck, my first hard dick… I guess it made me get one too, or something, because I felt like reaching down and putting my hand in my shorts. My uncle was over me, he was almost lying on top of me and he started sticking his dick up the little space between my shorts. I could feel it rubbing on my leg. He was pushing it more and more up there and then it squirted — yeah, right up my shorts! I thought it was piss, that I pissed myself or something. But my uncle just jumped off me and I was lying there thinking I wet myself, fuck, why'd that feel so good…"

John stopped. He was rubbing his face with his fingers.

"It's weird to tell you that. That's fucked up shit, huh Mira?"

"No."

"What? You don't think that's weird?"

"No."

"Wow. You're the first one, then. If I ever tell a woman that story, she just kind of freaks out and thinks I'm gay or something."

"No," I said again, because I didn't know how to say that I just didn't think anyone said stuff like this completely out loud. I wanted to know more, like did it happen again? Did this guy and his uncle ever actually have sex?

John threw his cigarette on the ground in front of us and wrapped his arm tightly around my shoulders. We must've looked like a couple.

"So what happened to you, baby?"

I laughed inside at him calling me that. Baby!

"Nothing. Nothing really, my cousin told me something…"

"What? How'd she say it to you?"

"It was nothing. I mean it was just him and some of his friends in our basement…"

"Sounds interesting." John laughed. "Come on, tell me."

"No, they were just telling me that sex happened between a mother and a father…"

"Yeah? Go on, it's all good."

I'd never actually said this to anyone.

"Go on, Mira, you can tell me." John started rubbing the back of my neck. "Remember all that stuff I just told you?"

"Well they told me about sex and it was weird because I never really heard anyone talk about it like that before, that's all."

I shrugged my shoulders. I didn't want John's arm on me anymore. But he held me harder when I shrugged.

"Yeah, Mira? So how'd they say it?"

Ezrah'd showed us pictures of sex: a mother and father kissing with their tongues. "The father's tongue makes her take off her clothes," he'd said. "Then the father puts his penis in the mother's vagina," Ezrah had started laughing the second he said vagina. "And when the baby comes out," he could barely finish his sentence, "there's a hole in her body the size of a head!" All the other guys had started cracking up, too.

"They all started asking me if I wanted a baby," I said.

"And what did you say?"

"No."

"You didn't want a baby?"

"No! Not from them!"

John laughed and I laughed, too. I think my voice finally sounded normal.

Suddenly, John turned my shoulders. We were standing in front of an old house with a cracked cement porch. The windows in front were covered with sheets.

"This is it," John said, unlocking the gate. "I want you to come in and see where I live."

"No, I can't. It's okay, I have to go."

"Come on, Mira. Just for a minute."

I told him no again, that I had to go home but he just kept saying: "It's okay, we're right here, just for a minute, just a minute." I really didn't want to. I didn't want to go inside that house.

John squeezed hard at the back of my neck. His hand felt so big, as if my whole head fit in it. I don't know why I thought that I couldn't just go home — run away from him even. I thought for a second that he might chase me if I ran. Or maybe he would've grabbed me around the neck so I couldn't breathe.

"One minute, come on. Just for a minute," John whispered. "I don't say these kinds of things to everyone, you know." He was shaking me back and forth a little by the shoulders. It made me hiccup one last time.

It smelled like smoke inside the front door. We had to go up a steep flight of stairs to another door at the top. John moved aside so I could go up first. I thought he was watching how I walked. I felt my hips move from side to side, even though I didn't usually walk that way.

He was going to touch me. As I climbed the stairs I knew what was going to happen. He was going to touch me.

"Thanks," John said quietly to the back of my head. "For coming up."

I thought again of running, but I was already at the top, waiting for his hands to come around and unlock the door.

It seemed as if the apartment was all in one room. There was a kitchen in one corner, a TV and a couch in another. There were videotapes all over the floor. It smelled as if someone had just been cooking.

I walked up to the window. There was a hole in the screen. I heard some kids screaming and I thought the noise was coming from that same big apartment building with the foil on the windows. I could still see it far off, standing like a rock. The sun was orange, just about to disappear.

"So this is where I live, baby."

John came up behind me and turned me away from the window. He was pointing to a couch. I squinted as I moved towards it. John was smoking again. I knew I should call home, but my parents were probably already out for dinner.

"Why don't you take off your shoes and get comfortable?"

John laid his cigarette in an ashtray on the coffee table. He stood in front of me and gently pushed me down on the couch. Then he moved the table back a bit so he could kneel on the floor. Smoke was filling up the room. I squeezed my thighs.

"It's okay," John said, sliding off my shoes. "I like you a lot, you know."

Holding my feet in his palms, John started sliding his fingers between my toes. I was sweating. I didn't want him to do that. I curled up my feet and tried to pull them away.

"Okay, okay. Anything you want, Mira," he said. But he didn't let go. He started kneading the arches of my feet with his thumbs. I let my head lean back and closed my eyes. It made me stop feeling like a sound was going to come out. My hands were on the couch beside my hips. I was bracing myself. It was like he knew something about me.

"You've got beautiful feet, Mira."

I lifted my head. John was pulling my toes up to his lips. I couldn't believe he wanted to do that! He was smiling, watching me try to watch him. My eyes kept opening and closing. I couldn't keep them open.

"Relax, baby..."

I felt my feet go all wet with his steam. A suction came down.

"Mmmmmmira..."

His slippery tongue pushed in and out of the cracks. My whole body started to shake. I thought for a second I was laughing with my mouth closed. John stopped and looked at me.

"You're a really funny girl, you know," he said.

John stood up and took off his T-shirt. There was no more sun in the room.

"I know you have a beautiful body under there."

My teeth were chattering. A beautiful body? I stared down at my smashed thighs. I heard the zipper of John's pants. My fingers were pushing under the elastic of my skirt. I wanted to do it and I didn't. I was wiggling around. My underwear slid off at the same time as my skirt. I knew I should call home.

"Oh man, that's sexy."

I felt my fingers behind me, unhooking my bra.

The father's tongue makes her take off her clothes. The father puts his penis in the mother's vagina.

"Oh God, yeah. You have beautiful breasts."

I stared at the hair above John's penis. His penis was starting to jerk around. It moved to the side, looking soft, then looking hard. It looked like a worm turning purple in the rain.

I wanted to get rid of the thing that was tightening inside me. I thought that if John just lay on top of me, everything would be fine. I knew what sex was.

"I could look at you like this forever, Mira."

My vagina started to feel strange on the couch, like powder dissolving into the ground.

"Aw, baby, why're you cold?"

John's body came down on me quick. His hairy chest pressed into my breasts. He was so heavy I didn't think I could breathe. I felt his penis start to move on my thighs, there was some kind of stuff on it, shiny, lukewarm. I was going to say stop, but John put his lips directly over mine. He was kissing me hard. His tongue was in my mouth. I was breathing out the side.

"Mmm, good, you really know how to kiss."

I started doing it like he was, it seemed like forever. I bit into his lips and he bit my lips back. John's hand wriggled down between both our stomachs. My legs spread wider. His finger poked around.

"Shhhhh, shhhh. Babe, you're so wet..."

I tried to look down between the darkness of our bodies. John's hand was holding the top of his penis. I moaned as he started to push it to my vagina. My moaning was there to keep the tiny space I had left between me and him. John was grimacing, wagging his penis up and down. He was pushing it deeper, then pulling it away. The head of his penis was shining with gloss.

"Open up baby, open your legs."

I knew it wasn't right. He was supposed to use a condom. But I felt myself plug. The plug made me mute.

John kept pushing and pushing, he couldn't go in any further. I didn't want the feeling of the tightness inside me. I wanted to break. John forced my knees open and whispered too loudly: "Open up, come on! Open up! Open up!"

One of my legs suddenly fell off of the couch.

"I'm inside you, babe. Come on babe, come on!"

Bone into bone. The plug was a wall.

John lifted his hands to the side of my head, used his hard shining forehead to keep me flat down. My eyelids were grinding.

"Good girl, shhh, good girl…"

I needed to move side to side in my hips. It felt different when I did it, different better. I pushed my hips up into his body.

"That's it. That's the way…"

Something was stuck there inside me, like a log stuck in fire.

"Yeah baby, fuck, good girl, that's the way…"

It didn't hurt more when I moved a bit faster. There was just something burning, a fever down there. John's hands squeezed my ass, his hands spread me open, spreading until I was bigger than tight… Oh God, I was doing it. It! Really It! I was feeling him move faster in and out. I was trying to feel every in, every out, but I couldn't keep up, it was going too fast. I didn't even know if I was feeling him or feeling me. I shut my eyes, I tried to relax…

"Yeah, fuck, you're so hot…"

Something flew up inside me. I heard myself grunt. It flooded my insides, flooded my head and I floated, floated, just for a second… Then his head hit my chest.

I was back in the room, back on the couch. John trickled out of me, saying my name.

"Mira! Mira!"

I was doing my trick: lying on the ground with my hands behind my shoulders, then pressing up, my back in an arch. I walked that way to the edge of the stage so that in front of their faces, my cunt touched the pole. It looked like a split-open flower they'd stepped on.

"Oh yeah, Mira! Go for it!"

I stood up red-faced and turned around slowly. I imagined their claps slapping right on my ass. I tried to smile backwards over my shoulder, but I could only do it for a second. It was a baby's smile, a dog's smile.

"We'll see you on the floor, sweetie!"

I ran downstairs right after I finished. Lani was smoking in the hallway before she went on. She passed me the butt, even though she didn't like me. A lot of the girls there never really liked me, so I couldn't ask them for a puff, even though I wanted one. All I ever needed was one puff.

It was disgusting for us down in the basement. Paint was flaking off the ceilings and it smelled like piss because the pipes were too hot. Adi was down there getting ready. I looked at myself beside her in the mirror. My eyes were starting to run. Sometimes I thought I looked good like that, right after I danced. But if I kept staring and staring, I saw this smeary-eyed slut. A girl whose head didn't even belong on her body, whose tits hung too low, whose legs were too big. I was one of those girls who shouldn't be up there, everyone knows it, she just shouldn't be there.

"Look at me," I said.

Adi was looking at herself.

"Look. I look disgusting."

Adi rolled her eyes.

"I look like an elephant."

"No." Adi laughed. "You don't know what it's like to be fat."

So why was I always looking down when I danced? Why did my tits feel like elephants' trunks?

Adi got up and came behind me. Her long skinny arms roped

round my waist. She stared at us both in the mirror, and said: "Up there, on your hands and knees, you put some kind of spell on them. Makes them go crazy!"

Adi could stop me from crying. Well, I wasn't really crying. Smoke always made me about to gush out. Adi whispered at my neck: "You look so good. Everyone knows."

I sat down and watched Adi finish herself. Her curly black hair was tied in two ponytails. She put baby blue eye-shadow high on her lids. All of it seemed so easy for her. I thought she must've known how to do this stuff forever. Makeup made her look even more beautiful.

Adi gave me a little kiss on the cheek before she left for upstairs. I tried to fix myself up, but I couldn't do it right. I was still shaky from the smoke. Grey blotches kept passing in front of my eyes. I put too much gunk in the grooves around my nose. All I had was a pink skirt and a red tank top in my locker. I never really matched but I didn't really care. I didn't think that the men cared either. If they didn't like what I was wearing, so what. I had high heels and big tits. Fuck.

Adi was the only thing that ever made me get back up there. I wanted to see her dance. The way she moved made it seem like nothing bad had ever happened in her body. Pushing away the floor with her feet, shaking her hips, smiling: "Come with me, come..." Adi's tongue slid in front of her teeth, you had to be quick to see how she did it, first coming out between her two lips, then curling over her teeth, licking: come. When she shook her ass at a guy, it was like she was in love with him. Her pussy out in front of his mouth, she'd hold his chin and practically feed it to him.

It was as if Adi had no fear. The way a vulture has no fear when it's eating the dead.

When I watched her dance, I knew I could do it too. Rush through the beat of those hundred white eyes, plow through the stink of their forced-back come. The men in tight circles, with gritting teeth and short breaths, moving their bottles up to their mouths.

"Mira! Mira!"

It all happened in slow motion. Those men didn't know if what they were looking at was real.

"Hey, I liked your dance, sweetheart," said the bald one in front of me. His stomach bulged out like a baby's.

"Sweetheart, c'mere."

The guy tapped his knee. I moved hip to hip towards him and turned myself around. I always showed them my ass right away.

"Yeah. I like that, darlin'."

I sat on his thigh and wiggled around, pretending to get comfortable.

"Yeah, shit! I like that."

I arched my back over the guy's gut and pumped my hips in time to the beat. I felt heat from the floor move up to my cunt.

"Name's Bill, darlin'."

I kept moving myself.

"How much for another?"

"Thirty."

"Alright, another. I like how this one moves."

There was a man at the table with Bill, a skinny guy who'd taken off his glasses. I saw his hands move underneath the table. Two of them, I was getting off the two of them! Bill started snorting behind me, telling me I was a wild girl. I thought for a second that the whole bar was watching my tits move up and down in my top, watching the way that my ass did a grind. I thought all the guys were going to gather around just to witness my cunt glistening.

"Wild, Mira, wild!"

I stood up and braced my hands on the table. I bent my knees deep and pumped back in his face.

"Oh man, shit she likes that!"

The bottom of the chain is the light in this place. The stink of the well is the light in this place.

I turned around quickly and raised my hands in the air. I was dancing now, just like Adi. I looked down at Bill's eyes. They were squinty and roaming. I put my hand on his chin and made him look up.

"I'm gonna take this wild one back to the hotel!"

"Don't do that," I heard the other guy say. "They have it right upstairs if you want it."

I'm shaking, I thought. All I'm doing is shaking.

"Naw. I want this one back at my place."

"I don't do that," I said, smiling.

"Yes you do, darlin'. How much you want?"

"I don't do that."

"Told you. She doesn't do that."

"How much?"

"No."

"Come on..."

"No."

"She thinks she's better than you, Billy."

"How much you want, wild one?"

"You can come to the back," I said.

"Yeah? What's at the back for a young guy like me?"

"Private dance."

"Alright sweetheart, lead the way."

"Oh boy, now you're fucked, Billy."

I turned on my heels, holding onto Bill's hand. It was soft and fat, all the fingers stuck together. I really thought everyone in the club was watching. "Alright Mira!" they shouted. "I'm next! I'm next!" The sound of my heels pock-marked the floor. A vulture, no fear, eating the dead.

In the booth at the back, I sat on the table. Bill slid in front of me, eyes at my crotch. Light pricked all over his face in white dots. I inched my panties down to my knees.

"That's it, sweetheart."

I started rubbing my clit around with two fingers. Bill followed my rhythm on the mound of his pants.

"That's it Mira. C'mon, how about a kiss?"

Still rubbing myself, I leaned close to Bill's face. He smelled like perfume, mixed up with beer. I pursed my lips at his torn-up beard. Then I leaned back and rested my ankles on his shoulders. I gave Bill a view. That's what he wanted, to see: that's how she opens, that's where I fuck.

All of a sudden, Bill gripped me hard by the waist. I slid off the table right onto his lap.

"I know you're a wild one!"

With me wedged in between the table and his gut, a tight little spot started to pulse in his crotch. Billy Bronco was trying to fuck! "Another song, sweetheart." The music kept pounding. "Come on darlin', you know what I like."

"Sixty," I said.

Bill breathed like a fool. I was jiggling, splayed open, trying to turn myself around.

"I see your pussy! What a pretty little pussy you got there."

My skirt was up around my waist. I undid my bra and let him pinch my nipples as I tried to settle on his legs. I was bouncing up and down. I wanted the cash.

"Yeah, lemme feel."

His hands moved to my ass. It smelled different in the room, like a match had just been blown out.

"There you go, lemme feel."

His finger was a slug.

"You're wet, sweetheart, yeah..."

"More?" I whispered, looking behind me.

Eyes screwed shut, Bill was nodding his head.

"Ninety."

"Yeah, just suck it, please."

His finger fell out of me.

"Kiss it, sweetheart, kiss it, please."

I slid under the table. Old cigarette butts stuck to my knees. I swam forward an inch through the walls of his thighs. I trickled some juice on him, forming a suck. I looked up at Bill. He was as hard as the floor.

Just a few sudden mouthfuls of cock and I swallowed his cash like the curse down my throat.

"Are you okay?" John was stroking my forehead.

I was giggling. I heard myself.

"Mira. C'mon, baby, open your eyes."

There was a candle making shadows on the ceiling. My back was glued to the couch. John was squeezed in beside me.

"What time is it?" I asked.

"It's okay, Mira, you just fell asleep."

I was covering myself with my arms. I knew I didn't fall asleep.

"Why were you just laughing, huh?"

"I have to go home." The whole room was flickering.

"Stay just a few more minutes," John said. He started drawing circles around my breasts. "You never finished telling me about your cousin, what's his name?"

"Who?"

"Your cousin?"

"Oh."

"Well…?"

"Ezrah."

John dipped a finger in me. "Wow, you're so wet."

"Stop!"

"You want me to stop?"

I felt buzzing in my body. Buzzing through my nipples and all down my legs.

"Okay, baby, okay."

John reached over me to open a drawer under the coffee table. He took out a thin cigarette and lit it from the candle. He started taking deep puffs. Then he put it between my lips.

I shook my head.

"Trust me, baby, it'll make you feel good."

I breathed in a bit but started to cough.

"Come on. Just a little more," he laughed.

I tried but it still wouldn't go all the way down my throat.

"Let me do something to you, Mira."

John looked up to the ceiling and took a deep suck of the cigarette. Then with his cheeks all puffed out he put his lips over mine. He blew such a huge blast of smoke down my throat that it inflated my stomach and went all the way to my vagina.

"Feel good?" John asked, sounding proud.

It smelled like him inside me.

"God, you look beautiful."

My mouth gaped wide. My eyelids were boiling.

"I mean it, baby. You look like a princess."

I started laughing. A Jewish American Princess!

"Shhh... Mira, tell me about your cousin. What was his name again?"

"Ezrah." I was dizzy.

"Ezzzzraaaaa," John yawned. "What kind of name is that? Hey baby, you okay? What kind of name is that?"

"Hebrew."

"You're Jewish?"

Tiny sharp prickling erupted in my wrists.

"My family."

"So you grew up that way?"

I nodded my head up and down too fast. It made me feel sick.

"Wow. Are you religious?"

"No!"

"Hey, hey sorry, I didn't mean to make you uncomfortable..."

I shifted around on the couch. I thought I might vomit on my back.

"Hey, come on baby," John whispered. "I just never met anyone Jewish before."

My body felt like it was buzzing full of bees. They were swarming inside the veins of my wrists, making my skin balloon out all red. I was biting the inside of my mouth to make it stop. Sour stuff coated the walls of my cheeks.

"Hey. Hey, Mira! I said I was sorry."

John was trying to turn me towards him. I didn't want to go. I shut my lips tight. But then he started stroking my arms softly and I felt a too-loud laughter coming on. It was like he was skinning me.

"What happened to you?" My nipples were raw. "When was the first time? Come on, forget about it, you're so wet, it's all good..."

My skin was breaking apart like a net. Each time he touched me the holes got so wide. It was hard to breathe right.

"Six. I was six."

"Really, six?"

"Yeah, six. I was sicks!" I started laughing and laughing. I was all made of holes.

"What happened? God, mmmmbabe, you're so wet."

John's big hand was a cup under my vagina. His other hand squeezed and squeezed on my tit.

"He and his friends made me go like their doggy."

God it was funny! Did I really say that?

John dropped his mouth to my mouth and pushed his tongue in me. I tightened. I sucked it. Sicks, I was sicks.

"Like the woman on her hands and knees in the pictures..."

John's fingers went up me.

The Joy of Sex!

"Shhh, babe, what's so funny?"

"All the guys stood around her in a circle."

John's fingers wiggled. I bucked my hips.

"Four of them were there."

Another finger inside.

"Ezrah went first."

John's hands slid under my ass.

"He came from behind."

More. Do it more!

"He felt my tits up under my shirt."

"Look how you're shaking..."

"They all did it after."

"Mira, spread wider."

John started moaning. His cock was so hard. My hand was around it. The heat split me open. John lifted my hips and turned me over like that. My stomach was down, my ass high behind me.

"How many, baby? How far did they go?"

I heard myself moaning. I felt myself wanting. Something to stop the holes from their spread. Ezrah loved *The Joy of Sex*. He stole it from his parents and hid it in the couch.

"Hey, come on, what's so funny?"

"They go: 'Mira, are you a doggy?'"

In the picture for "orgy," the woman was drawn on her hands and knees and four guys around her were squeezing her tits, holding her hips, pushing her ass. Ezrah called the woman a doggy. Like I want it now. Doggy! Doggy!

"You love getting fucked on your hands and knees."

More. Push it more. I want it harder, more! If it hurts, I don't care!

"Shit, you know how to move. Sexy little girl. How'd you learn how to move?"

John was splitting my ass, watching my breasts jiggle. Wind screamed through the window screen.

"Yeah fuck, baby, fuck it."

Fast up and down. There was thunder behind me. I felt my own body shoot out of my body.

"You like it there, don't you?" Ezrah called me once ranting in the middle of the night. "You want to stay in that fuckhouse. I bet all the guys who come to you love how you do it. They'd never get a girl like you anywhere else. Fuck, Mira, I bet they love how much you want to do it with them. Are you like some kind of dirty little girl when you fuck?

"When did you know that guys liked how you looked? When they looked at your tits? When they stared at your ass? When all my friends looked, you liked it. I knew you did. God, it's disturbing.

"I bet you love it when a guy says he wants your ass, you want to hear things like that, don't you? God it's so disturbing.

"You think after they leave it'll all disappear? That you'll be normal again? That you're the same old Mira? Fuck, I can't believe it! You dance for every dumb bastard who comes to you, don't you? You don't know the difference between us, do you? What's wrong with you that you don't know who's who?"

Ezrah knew I was scared of being alone.

In the summers when we were kids we used to walk in the ravine near my house, where the darkness of trees made the sun disappear. I'd pick flowers on those paths while Ezrah screamed up at the branches to freak out the birds.

He never wanted to hold my hand. Whenever we held hands it was because I made him pretend. I used to think I would be Ezrah's wife.

One day we walked further than we'd ever been before. I kept saying that we should turn around, that we were going to get lost, that we should turn around now, when suddenly Ezrah bolted from me, laughing: "I'm leaving this place! See you, Mir! I'm leaving!"

I was glued to that spot full of mushrooms and leaves. I was scared for him lost, scared for me lost, both of us lost in the forest forever. What were my mom and his mom going to do? Flies landed on my shoulders and I swatted them off hysterically. I couldn't make any noise.

I looked down at my feet and started shuffling backwards. I went so slow because I was hoping that Ezrah would come running back towards me. I kept turning my head in case he jumped out behind me. Black rubber branches touched the sides of my face.

I realized that my whole body was moving in slow motion because

I was waiting for something around me to change.

When I finally made it back to my house, our mothers were stretched out in the sun and Ezrah was there. I couldn't believe it. His arms were draped around his mother's bare shoulders. He was smiling at me with his top row of teeth. I thought he was saying: "See, Mir? You see? I know how to get home without you."

My mother gave me a hug and said, "Beautiful flowers." But the stems of the buttercups were squashed in my grip, their tiny heads all looking down limp.

Ezrah stayed over at our house that night. We slept together on the bed in the den. My stomach hurt. I was still so mad about how he took off on me. I was pretending to sleep when Ezrah snuck out of our bed. He came back a few seconds later with the flashlight from the kitchen. Then he pulled the covers over our heads and shone the light upwards.

"This is our new house," he said, matter-of-factly. "We'll stay up all night like this."

Ezrah had grabbed my comic book from the floor and was shoving it in my face. I shrugged and sat up with him. After a few stories, though, I started complaining like I always did that two girls would never fight so hard over the same guy. Two girls hardly ever want to kiss the same guy.

"Two guys want to kiss one girl," Ezrah said. "So what does it matter if two girls want to kiss the same guy?"

"It's not the same thing," I told him. "These girls are supposed to be in grade nine but look at their tits! No girl in grade nine would have tits like this!"

Suddenly, Ezrah snatched my comic book and wrecked our tent. He got on top of me and wrestled my arms over my head.

"What do you know about grade nine tits?"

"Stop it! Get off me!" I yelled, laughing.

Ezrah put his hand over my mouth. "They'll hear us! Shut up!"
His hand smelled salty and I stopped squirming.

"Tell me you're sorry," he said.

"Fine," I said through his hand.

"Tell me. Then I'll get off you."

"I said I was sorry!"

Ezrah eased up off my gut. His pajama pants looked weird, like a button was coming off. He lay down beside me and kept crossing and uncrossing his legs. He pulled the covers up over our heads again and stood the flashlight between our faces.

"Let's stay up all night tonight," he said.

All I felt like doing was looking at his face. The haze in the blanket made his eyes huge and grey. Ezrah was catching his breath, letting me stare. Right between his eyebrows, his face started changing. First his eyes got bigger, then his eyebrows pointed up. Ezrah looked like a fox. Then he turned into a clown with black lines on his skin.

Ezrah complained that I'd never stay up all night with him.

"No, I'm awake," I told him. My eyes were half-open.

It bothered me that I could never remember the second I fell asleep. I wanted to memorize that exact click. I knew most people died in their sleep and that meant going to sleep without ever waking up. I thought that if I remembered the exact second before falling, I would know for sure I wasn't going to die.

I kept hearing that song some kids sang at school: "If I should die before I wake I pray the Lord my soul to take, if I should wake before I break…" I couldn't remember the right words…

"Mira, you're falling asleep."

Ezrah set the flashlight at the top of our heads. A soft yellow circle touched the ceiling through the blanket. I asked Ezrah to tell me what was happening on my face.

Ezrah reached out and touched a spot above my eye. "It's okay to go to sleep," he said. He stroked my eyelid down.

My face felt so hot. I reached out my finger to do the same thing to him: a little, light stroke in the space above his eye. We each had one eye open, one eye shut. He kept touching my eyelid and I kept touching his. Our thin purple skins there rippled together.

Right before I awoke, I felt Ezrah's breathing, humid on my lips. I rolled on my back and took the blanket off my head. From the blueness in the room, I knew it was near morning.

I think I can remember every moment when I touched him or he touched me, because something always happened afterwards. It was as if I could feel more things under my skin, as if there was a night light searching my whole stomach. See, I liked it when Ezrah touched me, but I just didn't always want it to get started.

I think maybe the difference between all those times is lost in a pile in my head. Or my thoughts are too lazy to keep my brain clean.

Still, I know the best times happened when night-time pressed us together, sweating.

Then Ezrah started wanting his friends to hug me too and we all started looking at these books, then magazines — two naked people on top of each other, three naked people inside of each other, his head there and her head there, his legs up and her legs down, tits and pussies, cocks and dicks, Ezrah's hands on top of me, more hands underneath. What other girl played these kinds of games? And who else didn't say anything after? I thought I was the only one.

Her face was as high as a moon above her neck. I saw her the second I walked into that place. Adi was sitting alone at the bar, looking at the ceiling in a kind of daze. She was wearing one of those shirts with only one arm, it was white and said 'lady' in small silver script.

I sat where I could see her out of the corner of my eye.

My friend Nadia came up and hugged me over the bar. She gave me a Coke she'd spiked with two shots of rum. She said the boss had just left, but that he'd be back in an hour and I should wait. She said: "He'll take one look at you and give you the job, just like how it happened with me." It was the summer right after I finished high school. I wanted to get a job, move out of the house, make money, live. I told my parents I didn't want to go to university right away. I told them I just needed one year off and then I'd go.

Nadia grabbed my wrist. "That girl over there's crazy," she hissed. "She's been drinking for hours. She was fucking waiting outside on the ground when I opened!"

I kept my head straight, pretending that I hadn't even seen her yet.

"Look what she's doing now! She's fucking crazy!"

Adi had two cigarettes sticking out of her mouth. She was looking straight at me, her lips trying to hold and smoke at the same time. I saw her long fingers tapping the bar. There was one cigarette for each of us.

Nadia started talking about her boyfriend, how she was going to break up with him because he always wanted her to give him blow jobs and she didn't want to swallow his come. She just liked to put the head in her mouth, not the whole thing because it made her feel like she was choking.

I stole another look at Adi. Her face was completely full of smoke.

30

She was smiling through it with shining teeth. I jumped off the bar stool. I don't even know if I walked or ran. But there I was standing before her tightly crossed thighs.

Adi handed me one of the cigarettes.

"Thanks," I said, embarrassed.

I didn't always smoke, but I felt like smoking with her.

"You know what happens here later?" Adi asked.

I shook my head.

"Guys who come to this place don't even know what it's for."

I laughed. Adi sounded harsh. She had some kind of accent, Russian maybe.

"No. It's true. You know what this place is for?"

"I don't know, the guys all think they're going to get laid or something."

"That's it. And the girls who come here don't even know what a real guy is."

"Yeah," I agreed. But the only other time I'd been here, Nadia had slipped me about five rum and Cokes and I got so drunk I gave some guy a blow job in the toilet. I cringed at the thought of that. He was disgusting, disgusting.

I realized Adi was looking me up and down. She reached out and grabbed the hand I was smoking with.

"Closer," she said.

It made me nervous.

Heat from the cigarette moved towards my fingers. I shuffled in towards her.

"You have good eyes."

Then Adi let go of my wrist and I dropped the cigarette on the ground. Her eyes were really big and dark, with these star-shaped gold slits. For more than ten seconds we were eye into eye. A cold feeling surrounded my face. I felt pulled to a stop in the middle of running. How long can we keep looking at each other like this? How long can a girl keep looking at a girl?

Then the corners of Adi's eyes narrowed. I think she was surprised that I didn't stop first. She turned away and banged on the bar. "Jack!" she yelled.

Nadia rushed over. She was looking at me funny. I felt so different all of a sudden with Adi.

"Two shots, kinky girl," Adi said, winking.

I tried not to crack up as Nadia walked away. Her top lip had practically moved up to her nose when Adi called her kinky!

"She's not kinky," I whispered. "She doesn't like to swallow."

Adi licked her lips. "Fucker. That's the best part."

Nadia set the two shots of whiskey on the bar. Adi took out a huge wad of cash from her purse and put down a fifty-dollar bill.

"Thanks," I said. "You don't have to…"

Adi sucked her teeth as she handed me the shot. "I got more money than you, baby."

Baby!

Adi held her shot high in the air. She leaned her head back and poured the whiskey from practically a foot above her mouth. Nadia returned with that same trembling in her lip.

"Mira, come talk to me before you leave, okay?" she said, as she gave Adi change.

Adi laughed and cleaned up the bar with a napkin. "Don't worry Kinky, Mira's gonna come. Go on, have your drink…"

Nadia pleaded at me with her eyes. I downed my shot. It felt so good. What the fuck was Nadia scared of?

"Her boyfriend probably comes to the club," Adi said, as she lit another cigarette. "This is the kind of craphole men don't know what they're doing in. They buy their beers and watch Blondie's hair stream down her back. Then they sit there to dream of pulling it out of the way while she's eating them."

Adi started laughing hysterically. I felt my cheeks turn red. I think I swallowed that guy's come in the bathroom. I know I didn't spit it in the sink. I think I just closed my mouth and swallowed.

"I only like a man who knows what he can get." Adi was staring at me again, eye into eye. "I only like a man who can tell me what to do."

This time it was me who looked away first. Maybe that's it, I thought. Maybe I like that too…

"Okay! Kinky, she's yours! I go to work now!" Adi shouted. She jumped off her bar stool and threw her cigarette on the floor. I was standing there like a fool, thinking: But I just got here, don't go!

"So you coming or what?"

"Where? I don't know…"

There was something about her neck. It kept tilting to one side. It was thin like a branch that would snap in the wind.

"Okay, that's it. You're coming."

Adi rubbed two fingers together. Money. She twisted her shoulders into her coat, a short white thing with fur on the collar. "It's better than this piece of craphole," she said as she nodded over at Nadia, who was trying not to look at us.

Adi had the skinniest legs I'd ever seen. They looked like ropes.

"You coming or not?"

I'd only had one sip of my drink and the shot but I was dizzy. In my head it was pounding go, go, go… Adi grabbed my hand and started pulling us towards the door. We ran out of the bar like that, with Nadia yelling after us: "Mira! What the fuck are you doing?"

God! The wind whipping. My hair whipping. Adi was crazy! She dragged us out into the middle of the road, and jumped up and down trying to stop a cab. Cars were beeping at us, swerving. "Fucking people in a city like this," Adi screamed. "You can't never get their attention!" I was pulling her to the sidewalk and she was pulling me back to the middle of the road. We were cracking up. She was stronger than me.

When a cab finally stopped, Adi didn't let go of me. Her warm body crashed against mine on the back seat. Adi was searching in the pocket inside her jacket. Then she leaned over the front seat to the driver. "You mind?" she asked him softly, showing him something in her hand. The guy just laughed. Adi's ass was in my face for a second. She had such a good body that it made me feel weird. I felt like a guy looking at her ass.

Adi rolled down her window. "I hate this shit," she said, lighting a joint. She smoked it for a while. Then she passed it to me.

"Is it strong?" I asked.

Adi sucked on her teeth. "You can take it."

The cab driver kept looking at us through the rear view mirror and smiling. It was like he'd had Adi a million times before.

We ended up in the east end of the city, down near the water where all the factories are. I was fucked from the smoke. My heart was skipping beats. Cars were parked all around our taxi.

Adi stepped out into the middle of lights. Her ankle melted before it touched the ground. She pulled me out. I felt her hot hand. Someone started honking. She yanked on my wrist.

Adi pulled me inside to a dark flashing room. A room full of mirrors, high ceilings, black walls. Girls writhed upwards humping on poles. Inside their mouths it was shining like sirens. I crushed my face into Adi's coat. She elbowed me off her. I couldn't breathe. I didn't know who it was in those mirrors. Men squatted in circles with beer in their crotches or girls with their nipples pushing through their bras. Those girls looked like wolves with

34

the hair all shaved off them!

"Bitches," Adi whispered. She held my hand tighter.

I was coughing. I thought it was to keep myself standing.

"Hey Adi, who you got there? Who's your little friend?" I saw this one guy staring at me like a hunter. "You bring her for me?"

The man had thick eyebrows. He held out his hand. It was massive, with veins jutting up above each knuckle. It was like he was already feeling my breasts.

"What's up? Not going to speak? Tell me, where'd you find her?"

Adi was dragging me past him too fast. Wait for a second! I wanted to scream. A man like that wants to get to know me?

I tried not to stare at the guy as we were passing but I felt like his eyes were filming my face. Suddenly we stopped — Adi bumped into some girl wearing a muzzle and a thong. The music turned into a woman's heavy breathing.

Quickly I looked up and kind of smiled. That man was a stone looking back at me.

His eyes were wild, too-wide, outlined with black — eyes that could slice a goat's neck and not blink. When he started to smile back at me, I really couldn't take it. I dropped my head and stared at his legs instead.

The two huge thighs shifted open a bit.

I thought the guy was telling me: Sit on my lap.

I got so wet just from standing there, thinking. I felt tinier and younger than anyone in the room.

Then the man turned both his palms up and showed me the basins of his grip. Come here, he signed. I felt the motions in my pussy. Come over here and sit on my lap.

I heard Adi getting in some kind of fight with the girl. I couldn't go over to him, though. I was paralyzed. I mean I wasn't far away, but I didn't even know him. He was telling me to come and I saw myself tripping, head down, mouth open in front of his bulge.

Adi started swearing. She was pulling me away. Sticky wet lines smeared between my thighs.

When I looked back, the guy was still smiling.

"Cocksuckers," she hissed. "They're all stuffed full of cock."

In the basement, girls were running around a small fluorescent room. They stopped to look up at us but no one said anything. I thought they all hated me right away. One girl started laughing, a sharp birdy laugh. Adi was handing me things: a short dress, shiny shoes. I was raising my arms, dizzy for a second. Again that girl laughed. God! Cover me! Then in the mirror I heard myself laughing, just like the bird: "Look at me. I can't!"

The dress was too small. My tits rubbed together, my thighs rubbed together, my lips rubbed together. I was fucked.

"This is what they like," Adi was putting lipstick on my lips. "This is how they like you." She brushed my hair, brushed my cheeks.

I just wanted to stay down there with her. Lie on the floor. Turn off the lights. Lie down and not move.

That was when she told me that all girls want to dance naked for men. All girls would do it. Every last one.

"Not every one!" I got high again laughing. I knew so many who would never do this, every last one who would never do this! They wouldn't even think it. They'd never show their tits.

"Listen," Adi said. "You find me a girl who won't take off her clothes after you tell her what you like, there's no girl like that. A girl who won't strip after you tell her you want to see her tits moving around and you tell her all you want is her ass to get shaking. Then you'll see how she wants it, how she'll do it for your friends... You just tell her you like her sexy hot body, that you like how it moves, that you like what it does, you tell a girl this and you'll see how she'll do it."

I felt Adi's breath steam up my forehead. "A beautiful girl like you, though, you've really got something. See, sometimes I'm lying when I say stuff like that. But with you, there's no lying. Really. No lies."

She thought I was beautiful? Why did she lie?

Me and Adi held hands as we went back upstairs. Sweat from her palm wet the middle of mine. I felt older as I was walking with her like that. Our hips were moving at exactly the same time.

Adi led me up near the stage and talked to someone behind a glass pane. Then we went over to wait at the side.

The girl onstage was folding herself in half. She was peering backwards at the crowd through the slit in her thighs, tensing her ass cheeks open and closed. It was like she was talking to the men through her ass. I thought she was telling them: "I'll squeeze you in my cheeks. It'll be the best feeling any one of you ever had! My asshole's strong, Fuckers! Come on! I dare you!"

"He said you could go after," Adi whispered, her lips near my neck.

It felt good with her there so I leaned back. She laughed as she took my weight. "You're funny, Mira."

I turned around and wrapped my arms around her. "I can't!" I moaned. My hands slid down her skirt.

I didn't want to tell her I was scared of that man. Scared that I wanted him or wanted this.

"You can, you can do it, I know you know too." Adi kissed me on the lips. The girl with the legs whipped by us and laughed.

"Go. Go ahead."

There was blood in my ears, I felt blood down my neck.

"Go Mira! Go!" Adi gave me a shove.

There.

There I was.

Standing over the men.

I was watching my toes all crushed up in the shoes. I hated those shoes. I tried to kick them off. I heard clapping below me. Strong lights overhead. Is this what she does? Is this how she does it? I felt myself moving. My hips were too loose. I felt my breasts bouncing bunched tight in the dress. God, I was stoned with my hair in my face. I wanted it to stop. Pull my tits from my body…

"What's her name?" someone shouted.

"Mira."

"Go on, Mira!"

My neck began moving.

"Mira! Mira!"

I looked at the ceiling.

"You're alright, sweetie!"

The dress was clumped like rubber at my hips. I was twirling around, reaching behind me.

"Yeah go for it, darlin'!"

"Take it off, hottie!"

"Jesus, check out the hooters on that little babe."

I was taking it off.

Get everything off me!

Then my hands hit the floor. My hands and my knees. I saw the dress under me black as a rag. Sweating, I'm sweating. My bra and my panties. I looked down between me, crawling away. Hundreds of eyes were there watching my ass. Animal, animal. "Look at that ass!" Beats shook the floor. I put my ear down. They all want to fuck me.

"What a hot fucking chick!"

My ass tilted higher for that one guy's eyes.

I was pulling my underwear tight up the crack. Yeah, you can fuck it. My ass for your eyes. All you can fuck it.

"Spank yourself darlin'!"

My hand made my ass red.

"Yeah, fuck, she's wild!"

God, I'm so fucked! Oh Fuck. You can fuck it. Flat on my face, humping the floor…

"She's hot!"

"A real 10."

"Kinky little chick."

I don't know how long I was down there like that. I was licking my lips when the thumps started changing. I pressed up to stand with the dress tight against my chest. There was wetness on my thighs, splinters in my face.

"When's she coming down here?"

"Yeah, I want a piece!"

I looked for the man out there in the pit. I wanted to jump straight into his hands. Down through the fire, thrown to the lions…

"Mira! Hey Mira!"

But the guy wasn't sitting where he was before. I stood there dumb, thinking: so, I am the lion! My mouth gaped in a grin. I ran off the stage and right into Adi.

"I'm not what those guys are used to, I'm not!" All of my breaths started to pour out at once.

"Fuck you, yeah you are! That was fucking hot!"

Suddenly, Adi kissed me, longer than before. My underwear was soaking wet. I felt myself opening, my tongue on her lips. I heard her sink a little moan into my mouth. We started frenching, our saliva was sticking. It felt pretty good just to play with her tongue. Adi's hands were sliding towards my ass. I was too wet. My teeth dug in her lips. She tasted like smoke. I bit down so hard that she pushed me away. I think she was shocked, she was covering her mouth, but I just started laughing. I mean I was laughing so much that she cursed and was trying to yank my dress away. I held it tight and I just kept on laughing, squealing...

When Adi realized that a few guys were watching us, she grabbed me by the waist and pulled me back close. I opened my mouth on her neck and I felt us shuffling over towards their table... Then we were kissing again, full-on making out, this time grinding ourselves into each other. I felt so hot that I let the dress fall. Adi squeezed the sides of my breasts. I think a few guys were closer around us. Someone undid the string of her bikini... I heard a guy whisper: "Keep going with her..."

Adi swirled her tongue in and out of my mouth as she pressed and rubbed her nipples into mine. I held her naked back. We were stepping on money, sliding on bills! Then Adi's hot nipple hit my mouth. She held my face down as I licked and sucked hard.

I wish it could've stayed like that longer. When I knew Adi liked me and I liked her too.

It was about fifteen minutes before we closed the next Saturday when John came back to the cafe. He was carrying flowers and he'd shaven. It was like he thought I was the love of his life.

I hadn't given him my number because I didn't want him to call me at home. I didn't want my parents to ask who he was. I took his number, though, and said I would call. He made me promise I would call. But I didn't. I couldn't. I felt too weird after I left that night. John had called me a cab, he'd even given me money for the ride and I started hyperventilating the second I got into the car. It was quiet, I mean, the cab driver didn't know, but I couldn't stop thinking: what'd I just do? I could still feel John's tongue pushing into my mouth, his tongue making all of the noises of sex. "Shit, little baby, you know how to move."

Seeing him standing in front of me again, all I could remember was his sandpaper tongue. And his purple hanging cock, how it swung from side to side. I remembered exactly how the whole thing went in me. Over and over, that feeling in my gut and the second time, how I wanted it to happen... But I knew I didn't want it to happen again! I didn't want him as my boyfriend in that house that stunk of meat.

John kissed my forehead. "Hey. How about the flowers?"

I put my face in the bunch of ribbon carnations. Their gross perfume made me think of my period. I'd gotten it in the middle of the night a few days after the sex. I bled so much that it went through to the mattress. My mother was mad. That was your grandfather's mattress, she said.

"You're getting off soon, right? I'll wait for you here. We'll go get something to eat."

John thought I was just going to go with him? That I was his girlfriend or something? He was standing too close to me. I wasn't even off work yet. I had to sweep the floor, mop it and put away the cash.

"I'm still busy," I said.

My voice sounded mean. I didn't mean for it to be so mean. I left the flowers on a table and started sweeping. My head was saying: leave, leave, leave.

"I'll wait."

John just stood there. I had to sweep around his greasy fraying jeans. Fucking leave! Just leave!

"Stop for a second Mira."

I looked up.

"What's the problem here, huh? Didn't you have a good time last week?"

His eye twitched and then widened. I really didn't want him to be here.

"I couldn't stop thinking about you, you know that, Mira?"

God! Stop saying my name!

I started sweeping again, moving behind the counter. I wished my boss would come up from the basement. I wished I'd never gone with this person. I wished I'd never done any of it.

John was following me. I heard him saying stuff under his breath. "I thought things had finally changed. I thought some things had finally changed…"

I was looking at his hands, his hands clenched in fists. I wanted to scream for my boss, or something, but I just stood there listening to John's jerky breath.

"You let me have you so much last week. You can't tell me you didn't like it. Remember how you were kissing me? You loved it. You can't tell me you didn't love it."

His fingers came open. They were coming out towards me…

John started laughing. "I'm not going to hit you, fuck! You think I'm going to hit you?"

No! But you were the one who started all this! You were the one who did everything, God, why'd I let you do all that stuff?

"You don't want to see me again, is that it? Huh? What kind of game you playing?"

I was watching the floor, still checking his fists. I just didn't want what was next. How much time do I have to be here? Look. Look what I got myself into…

"What, you're not going to talk to me? Who do you think you are? Some good girl, huh? Not by a long shot, baby. I've been around and I can tell you that. You gave it to me, Mira. I've seen how most girls are and you were willing, yeah. Other guys are going to want you to go with them, too. They can tell you're the kind who'll open good, you know. They just look at you there and know. You know that, too, huh, don't you? Well, no one's gonna do to you what we did, I can tell you that. I've been around. I've seen how things are. You're a rare bird, baby..."

John reached out and stroked my face. I didn't flinch. "Fuck you're probably gonna end up sleeping with any guy who says a few nice words to you. You're a real little sex fiend you know that? Yeah, you know that… Fuck, I've never been with a girl who got as wet and horny as you did, Mira. You could probably take ten guys at once!"

John's hips started moving back and forth. His hands looked like they were holding my ass. "Yeah I could get Michael and the guys and we'll come for you after work, follow you home… We can just have you there in your daddy's backyard, yeah, doing the train… And you'd probably moan exactly the way you moaned with me, 'Oooh, wait, wait, oooh...'"

"Fuck off! Just fuck off!"

"Mmmm, wanna hit me? Is that it? You want to hit me?"

I raised the broom from the floor.

"Yeah, smack me with it. Do it. Smack me."

John closed his eyes and puffed out his chest. His lips had turned white. I lifted the broom up over my head. I wanted to knock off his head.

"Fuck you! I hate you!"

John eyes bolted open as the broom hit his head. Into his ear and into his face. He started swatting it away but I just kept on smacking. I heard weird grunts from the back of my throat. I was breaking through skin. I wanted to do more.

But I stopped when I saw he was cradling his face. Light red blood was dripping through his fist. When John saw the blood, it was like he got happy. He started laughing with his jaw open and practically singing: "A slut, a slut, a good-time fuck, the kind of fuck that's yours for free..."

We heard the sound of my boss coming back upstairs. John spit on the floor at my feet and ran.

Everyone believed me when I told them I worked the night shift, data entry. My family did, anyway. I told them I liked the people I worked with and that the money was good. I mean how much does anyone really want to know anyway?

The only one who I ever told the truth to was Ezrah.

We hadn't seen each other in a while because he was away at school. I hadn't seen him that much since the first year of high school, actually, because his family had moved up north and we'd stayed downtown. We just saw each other on holidays. It was Yom Kippur when I told him. We were in the back seat of his brand new car.

We used to hang out in his parent's car all the time on holidays when we were kids. Sometimes I stayed inside synagogue longer than Ezrah because I liked hearing the people singing, that wailing coming out of their nostrils.

Ezrah still made fun of me for wanting to stay. "Being a good little Jew?" he asked when I got in the back seat with him.

"No. I don't understand what they're saying."

"Yeah? That's because it's in Hebrew."

"I know, stupid, but it still bugs me. You'd think I would understand something after all this time."

"Why?" Ezrah stared at my dress.

"Because what's the point of being there if you don't understand anything? What's the point of standing up and sitting down if you don't understand?"

"You're not supposed to."

"You are too. People understand when they go to church."

"Whatever, Mira. You want to go to church?"

"I would understand it at least."

"No you wouldn't. You're Jewish."

"Because our family is."

"No, because you are."

"Well I'm not. I don't feel it."

"That's really fucked up, Mira. You know what the Jews have been through to survive? You know how amazing our religion is? Don't fucking say that."

Ezrah always acted the same. Ezrah always looked the same. It was something about his eyes, he always scrunched them up to sound moral. I wasn't going to be Jewish just because he made me feel guilty. I knew there was something I was really supposed to feel. What was the point of doing it all if I didn't ever feel a thing?

I assumed everyone else felt something when they were in the temple. Something like a bird whipping around and round their head. Or maybe they felt that God was a man giving them mouth-to-mouth resuscitation. Or maybe God was the bird swooping up to the rafters that talked to them as they stood up and sang.

"Keep singing for me, Sir. Keep singing for me, Miss."

God's voice would be deeper, more urgent than theirs.

"I'll watch you, Man. I'll protect you, Woman. Just keep rocking back and forth."

Isn't that the only reason why people would do it every Saturday? Because they felt God breathing or flapping around them? So that they could feel some real presence dropping into their heads? I knew that the feeling of God would have to exaggerate things like this. Until there was some kind of needy hole in the system — like the beak of the baby bird waiting for its Mama, shrieking until she drops nourishment through. If you prayed every day you developed this hole and God would stick a little tongue through. Ezrah reached into the front seat and put on the radio. "I want you to come and visit me at Thanksgiving. You should really meet some of my friends, Mir."

"Will you shut that off," I snapped.

Ezrah turned the radio off and looked at me. "What's wrong with you?"

"Nothing."

Then silence.

"What the fuck is up, Mira?"

"You look like you're working hard these days," I said, changing the subject. "What's up? You a doctor yet?"

"What's up, you have a boyfriend yet?"

"Fuck off. None of your business."

"So what are you doing then? My mother said computer-something?"

"Yeah."

"Where you living?"

"East end."

"Gross. Why there?"

"I like it."

"I don't believe you. Why way out there?"

"It's probably better than your crappy little room in a dorm."

Ezrah laughed. "Shut up."

"So what are you doing these days besides studying?"

"Studying."

"That's it?"

"Yep."

"No girls?"

"No girls."

"I don't believe you."

"It's true."

"I bet there's some good-looking girls in your class."

"They're alright."

"What? No one you like?"

"No one like you."

"Oh come on!" I was smiling at him. His legs looked too long for the back of the car. I was uncomfortable in my dress. It was low-cut. I had a shawl wrapped around me.

"Let me see you."

"No."

"Why not?"

I let the shawl fall down my shoulders. I shifted a bit on the seat so that my body was facing him.

"You look good."

I looked down.

"So what are you really doing now?"

"I feel weirded out telling you."

"Why?"

"I don't know. Just do."

"Why?"

"Stripping."

"What?" Ezrah turned his body away from me. "Fuck!"

Both of us became silent. I could tell he was thinking of what to say next without making things worse. But his lips were shut so tight it was hard for him to get it out.

I wanted to touch his arm or something. "Don't be like that, come on…"

"Why the fuck are you doing that?"

"I don't know…"

"No. You don't know? Fuck, how can you do that?" He was disgusted with me. It was sliding out of him easier now.

"It's what I'm doing right now. I don't know. It's not a big deal."

"What the fuck Mira, it is a big deal. How can you actually do that?"

"Because, I don't know, it's in me. I don't know. That's how I can do it."

"What are you talking about?"

"I mean… I don't know. I mean, maybe I was meant to do it."

"No. You really fucking believe that?"

"I don't know. Yeah. Maybe it was something people always said to me."

"Who? Who said it? Guys said that to you?"

"No. Sometimes…" Were you always this disgusted with me?

"That's embarrassing, fuck. I don't how you can do that."

I didn't want to talk to him anymore. I didn't want to say another word. Suddenly Ezrah turned around and stared at me. He was looking at my cleavage.

"I'm going to come and see you."

"No you're not."

"Yes I am."

"No you're fucking not!"

"Any dumb bastard can go see you naked? So? So can I."

"Fuck off." Fuck you. Ever since we were kids. Fuck you.

Our breaths were filling up the car. I opened the window and heard a song coming out of the synagogue. I knew it was the last one. A bunch of people all crying together, not wanting to die.

"It's almost over in there," I said.

Ezrah got out of the car and left me. I watched him walk through the big wooden doors of the temple.

I felt like laughing for a second. I didn't even tell him the whole thing. That after a while I didn't even think the men were that bad. That I'd had their fingers up me. That I let them kiss my breasts. That they'd fucked me, sucked me, stroked my head.

I stayed in the car until I saw my family come out of the synagogue with the crowd. My father and mother had circles under their eyes. Ezrah was there, talking to my mother. I didn't care. I hated him then. He looked tired and mean, just like his dad. As I watched him with my family I was thinking about later that night, about getting stoned and dancing at the club with Adi. I wondered what she would think of Ezrah. Of me sitting in the car with him, atoning for my sins.

Adi made all the arrangements for us to move upstairs. I did it because I needed a place to live. After a few months at the club, I'd made pretty good money and Adi said that we'd make a lot more if we lived up there. I usually made at least $150 per shift and always extra if I did stuff in the back. Adi said that the girls who took guys to their rooms could make over $800 a night! Management took 35% at the end of the week, plus $150 for laundry and phone. I thought that was a lot, but Adi said we could stiff them a bit, pretend like our tips were smaller than they were and just give 35% on the standard fees — $75 for a blow job, $150 for full service.

I didn't think so much about what it would be like living up there when I said yes. Making big tips was part of the thrill of the whole thing.

The day we moved in, I waited in a little area outside the office with my stuff while Adi got our keys. I wanted to know how she got into dancing, but it always seemed like a stupid question right before I was going to ask.

After a few minutes, a guy stuck his head out of the office. He looked at me like something was wrong with my clothes. I'd never seen that guy at the club before. He was short and thin, with brushed-back black hair. I opened my mouth to say something or smile, but he just turned and closed the door. I imagined him saying to Adi: "What's she doing here? What's she got to do with you?"

I didn't want to meet that asshole. I was glad Adi knew what to say to him.

But when she came out of the office, she wasn't looking at my eyes. She just linked her arm through mine and we headed up the stairs. I noticed a few of the girls hovering up at the top, but they had disappeared into their rooms by the time we got up there.

I didn't expect that it was going to be so much like a regular hotel, a regular craphole hotel. The stucco walls were gray with dirt. Sheets were heaped outside the doors. Our rooms were right beside each other: 221 and 223.

"Don't worry," Adi said to me as she handed me the key. "We'll be out of here in a few months."

But right away it was worse than I'd imagined. I felt like I'd just arrived at a place where girls were carcasses filling a field.

I remembered when John told me he wished I was in California porno. "Nothing to be ashamed of, Mira," he'd said. "You sure got the tits and ass for it."

It didn't smell so bad inside my room. Someone must have just sprayed perfume. But in the bathroom there was a clump of black hair down the drain of the sink. The plant hanging in the shower had wilted brown vines. I unhooked it and gave it some water. The soil was filled with tiny white balls.

In the bedroom, two mirrors faced the bed. One of them was full-length. My window overlooked the parking lot. There were a few trucks out back. For the first time I noticed that there was a park down the street from the club, at the end of all the factories. It looked like a high green hill with trees on top. I couldn't tell how far it went back. I was standing there staring when the streetlights turned on.

I went over to Adi's room. She was putting her stuff away in the drawers. I'd told my parents I was moving into a friend's apartment, so I didn't really bring that much stuff. Just two big bags of clothes, some books and some shoes.

"You're already finished unpacking?" Adi asked without turning around.

When I didn't say anything back, she said: "Don't worry. Everything's fine."

I sat down on the edge of her bed. She still hadn't looked at me. For the first time I felt like she wasn't telling the truth, that nothing was fine, that she'd been doing this for years.

"What'd that guy downstairs say about me having a room?"

Adi kept wiping her hands off on the bedspread in between unpacking her clothes.

"Nothing. He said nothing. It's all fine."

"Really, what'd he say?"

"You have the room, don't you?"

Adi was setting up her makeup by the table and mirror. When she finished, she turned on the TV. Then she propped herself up against a pillow at the top of the bed. I climbed in beside her. I felt like talking but I didn't know what to say. I didn't know if I felt bad or if she felt bad or which of us was worse. I took her hand. It was cold. I kept moving my fingers around, squeezing, trying to say something about the place, but it wouldn't come out. We just stayed on her bed like that, eyes glazed over, watching TV. I fell asleep on top of the covers.

When I woke up, I didn't know where I was. My neck was twisted and my muscles hurt. I turned to look over at Adi. She was still sitting up. The TV was on but she'd turned off the sound. Her eyes were wide open but it looked like she was sleeping.

I slowly rolled my head until it was straight. I just wanted to be still. I wanted to keep my body still.

Ezrah said: "Sit on that chair with your arms behind your back. You going to do it for me, Mir? God, your breasts got so big. I bet you've never had a guy say that he didn't want anything but your breasts. How do they say it? I don't want your pussy, I just want your titties... I don't know how to say it, Mir, c'mon, do it. I love your breasts. You remember that time at the table with our parents? I know you remember. I couldn't stop looking at you in that top, that tight green top you wore before you got a bra. You pushed them out for me, I know you did. Your nipples got hard because I was looking at you there. And I was trying not to look because I couldn't eat the fucking meatballs! My mother kept dishing them onto my plate: 'Why aren't you eating? You don't like my meatballs?' No, I'm not eating meatballs, Ma, because Mira's tits are right in front of my face! God I wish you never got a bra. I wish all girls never had to get bras. I love your breasts. I love how they grew. I love how they hang, the nipples are so red. Do it for me Mir, put your hands behind your back. Push out your tits. Just like you did at the table. You knew what you were doing, wrapping your arms round the back of the chair, arching your back, shoving your perfect tits in my face. I swear I wanted to crawl under the table... Sorry, I can't eat meatballs right now, Ma — Mira's in my mouth, Mira's on my face!

"Fuck, what would you do... I bet my father and his buddies would go to that place. What if he walked in? What would you do? Uncle Morris comes in and pays to see your tits? Fuck it's disgusting, I can't even think about it. 'Hey, you've got big hard hooters, baby!' Is that how they say it? 'Lemme see your tits. Lemme buy that tit a drink.' God, it's disturbing. I'm really disturbed. I love your body better than any fuck could. I could suck you for hours, suck every inch. Until you had breasts all over your chest, nipples in rows sprouting all the way down."

John was at the cafe three weeks later. I couldn't believe he came back. I guess I felt a bit strange about what happened. I mean, at first I was relieved when I thought I'd never see him again, but then I felt bad. I thought: what if I was wrong? What if I was wrong to be so upset? I couldn't believe I hit him with the broom! Why exactly had I been so mad?

John didn't look at me when he ordered a coffee. He didn't give me a tip either.

I thought: just be nice to him even if he isn't nice to you.

I went to clean off the table where he was sitting and tried to say hi. I even said his name. I don't think I'd ever said his name before. John just shrugged. He didn't look good. He was smoking and looking out the window. I felt like I had to make things better.

"Come on, John, how are you?"

He looked up at me with soupy eyes. For a second I thought for sure he was going to cry. I had to make it better right away.

"John…"

"What?"

It wouldn't come out of my mouth.

"What, Mira?"

"I don't know…"

"Yeah? What do you want to say?"

"Nothing. I mean, I feel bad about last time."

John reached for my little finger and squeezed it. He butted out his cigarette and then took my whole hand.

"We're gonna be okay. It's all going to be okay."

I didn't want him to say that! That's not what I meant. I just wanted to make sure he was okay. God, I didn't want him to say that! I smelled the smoke and the coffee wafting off him.

John waited for me outside after work that day. He was standing there grinning with his hands behind his back. I thought: I am the one who's done it this time. I didn't leave it alone. I made this happen.

We walked back to his place in silence. My stomach was a mess. He'd cleaned up a bit in there. It didn't smell as meaty as the last time, either. I sat on the couch. John sat down beside me right away.

"I've got to say it, Mira…"

I was staring out the window.

"You look beautiful. I mean it. You are a beautiful, sexy girl."

"Stop."

"What? Hasn't anyone ever told you that?"

"Not like that."

"Like what?"

I glanced over at him. "Looking like you do and saying that."

"You mean looking at you like I want to kiss you?" he asked.

I squeezed my lips together. I couldn't stop them from turning up into a smile.

John slid close to me and took my face with his hands. His skin was dotted with sharp black hairs. Suddenly his tongue was everywhere in my mouth. I tensed my thighs. I was letting this happen all over again.

John pulled away first. Our lips came apart with a loud pop. My mouth felt like it was hanging from my face.

"Now you look even more... You really look like a princess. Look I'll show you how beautiful you are, just wait."

John jumped up and turned on the TV. He got out a video camera that was behind it. I just sat there staring. I didn't really want to think about what I was doing. My body was beating from that kiss. I didn't want to be on this couch for so long...

"I want to show you something. This'll be quick. Hang on, there... You see? Wait…"

John was hunched down behind the video camera. It was a bit easier to look at him when his face was covered. "You see yourself, Mira?"

I was on the TV, leaning back against the couch. I'd never seen my face on a TV screen before. My cheeks were red. My lips were kind of open. That was what I looked like? That was how he saw me?

"See how beautiful, baby? Look." John told me to shift over to the left and relax my legs a little. "I'm not taping this, okay? I'm just showing you how pretty you look."

I didn't recognize myself. I thought I looked older than fifteen. I put my finger in my mouth and bit it to stop myself from saying out loud: "Do I really look like that?"

"Yeah baby, like that, that's good," John was focusing in with the camera so that my head was at the top of the screen and my knees were at the bottom. The back of the couch was shining behind me.

"Mira, you're a natural." I saw John's cock pushing up inside his pants. "I gotta show this to Mikey. He's going to love this..."

I watched my legs shifting on the screen. Am I sexy? Would every guy think so?

"Why don't you take something off and get comfortable?"

"Who's Mikey?"

"My uncle. Michael. Take off your shirt."

My fingers were moving in between my buttons.

"Why's your uncle going to love this?"

"Because he's smart. He's going to love it, don't worry, he's going to love you…"

I thought right then that I was at John's so that something would happen, something I wouldn't ever do by myself.

"That's it Mira, that's the way."

I wanted him to keep talking.

"That's sexy, baby. Just a bit more, take off some more."

I was out of my shirt. I sat there in my bra. The straps were making red marks on my shoulders. I touched the top of my breasts and dropped my finger down the crack. I kept wanting to see my finger disappear. My nipples got hard. John started going in close-up on my stroking.

"Look how pretty your tits are. Look."

My nipples were itching inside my bra. They looked so big. I'd never seen them that big. I rubbed them through the fabric. I wanted to put them in my mouth.

"That's it, touch them. Pinch them. Fuck, that's good."

I had one in each hand. I was squeezing and twisting. I heard John breathing behind the camera. "Move your hand now, babe." He was telling me what to do. "Touch yourself lower. Touch your pussy. Look at yourself."

I saw my face changing, my mouth getting bigger. I couldn't stop licking the corners of my lips.

"You look so fucking sexy."

My bra was hanging from my arm.

"That's it, take it off. Good girl, take off your skirt."

I didn't know if I wanted to see what it looked like down there. Everything felt so big and rushing.

"You are a fucking sexy girl."

Hairs in thick strokes were covering my vagina. A dark brown line separated the two parts that were sticking softly to each other.

"Hang on."

John took his face away from the camera. He was setting up a tripod, taking off his pants.

"I gotta show you something."

Crouched behind the camera again, I watched his big stomach, the beef of his legs. John started focusing in on my vagina.

"Stop it. Don't!" My voice got high-pitched. I covered myself with my hands.

"Easy." John laughed. "Just wait. I'm not taping it. You'll see how pretty it is. You'll see what I see."

"No. I don't want to."

"Yeah you do, baby. You've got the prettiest pussy. All I can see is that pussy in front of me. I dream of it at night, growing over my face."

There on the screen were my thighs, all that hair... John came over and kneeled on the ground. I wanted to slam my legs shut and double my hands. I turned my head to the side and held hard.

"Open your eyes."

Slowly, squinting, I looked at the screen. John's thick fingers moved my slippery hand. He was trying to spread me. The whole screen was moving with red and pink dots.

"See how hot it is? You've got such a beautiful wet pussy, Mira."

I strained my eyes. A beautiful pussy? I wanted to hurl like a brick through the screen!

"I want to show you how it looks."

No! I'll never get used to what that looks like.

I was holding his fingers right where they were sliding. I couldn't help looking down. My vagina stuck onto the fingers of a man.

"Your pretty wet pussy."

There was foam on John's hand. I looked up at the screen. There was something about all the skin, pink and stretched — it looked like a bat hanging upside down!

Quickly, John leaned in and placed his head between my thighs. He stuck his tongue deep up my vagina and started really frenching me there. I watched the back of his head on the screen: he was pushing and licking me all around the hole. The muscles of his lips were curling inside me. I couldn't stay still. He was sucking all my wetness. It was making me sweat.

"Stop, stop…" I heard myself moaning.

John spread my legs wider, then he stopped and pulled away. He looked back at the screen.

"Don't you see how sexy that is?"

Still watching the screen, John pushed his finger up me. I was so wet that his finger disappeared. He was holding my thighs, making my lips flare. Another finger went in. Then there were three. It wasn't going to stop. This was never going to stop. Heat rose between my shoulder blades, two red-hot rods. I stared at the screen. All his fingers were wiggling inside me. I bucked my hips up into his thrusting. It was never going to stop. It was never going to stop.

"That's it, Mira, watch yourself fuck."

The hips of me fucking. I couldn't stop fucking! I couldn't stop moving in time to his jabs. I felt more, I felt more, God, just one second more filled up on his fucking, all of me there...

"Look at you, baby. Look at yourself."

I stared at my pussy, his hand was inside it, stretching me naked, fucking me harder. I watched myself shaking, my pretty wet pussy, his thick fingers jabbing so hard I was huge! God I screamed and sucked in!

Shuddering, I was shuddering.

I imagined that she was the mother and I was the daughter, with all those eyes on us, calling our names. We both wore red dresses with white around the edges. I licked her breasts. She stroked my head. She was the mother and I was the daughter. Her arms wrapped around me.

"Suck her, Mira, suck her!"

We got down to the floor. I was lying on my back. Adi was above me, shaking her hips. She was spreading herself open under her dress and I saw for a second a wheel at my eyes. It was a bright red circle that was rusted inside: that was her pussy. It was nothing like mine.

Adi told me she never wanted to have children. I didn't believe her at first, or maybe I'd just never heard a girl say that. But when she told me she was thirty-one, I was shocked. Really, thirty-one? You can't have a baby too much longer after that. There was no way Adi looked thirty-one! She was doing all this stuff at thirty-one?

I raised my arms. I held on to her waist. I wanted her to come down and sit on my face. It was like a wheel was spinning out from her centre. I wanted to stick my tongue through the spokes. Come down some more! I wanted to scream. But Adi just kept hovering over my mouth, dipping down for a second, then shaking up.

She told me there was this guy who came to the club to try to make her pregnant. She said he wrapped her legs around his back and held them in a lock while they fucked.

You don't always use condoms? I asked her. I didn't believe it.

Depends on the guy, she said, depends how I want it.

"Sit on her face, Adi! Squash Mira's face!"

The yelling of men. Lights circling above us. It tasted like crying inside my mouth.

He was the one who stopped wanting it, she told me. He stopped wanting me to come. The only guy I ever wanted stopped wanting me to come.

"Yeah, Mira! Lick it!"

Her back and forth ass, her back and forth hips. She finally split open, sank hard on me there. A cunt full of pieces was stuck in my mouth. I just wanted to keep doing it, I wanted to take the weird pain from her there, suck it all dry so she couldn't wail. I wanted to know that she still felt good. It didn't matter if some guy didn't want to make her come! We were showing a whole roomful of guys what sex really was! Sex is the animals licking and cleaning, mother and daughter in front of a crowd, making each other come, tears sliding down their throats, going and going and groaning from their guts: This is love! It doesn't matter how we got it!

Me and Adi never talked after shows — one of us was usually busy with a guy. We talked around noon, when we got up. But Adi came to my door later that night. She was wearing a light purple slip. I knew she'd just smoked.

She lay down on top of the covers, close to me. "I've never done that before when I was working," she said.

"Done what?"

"You know."

I'd brushed my teeth but she was still there.

"I'm not right down there."

My eye kept steady on a crack on the wall.

"No..."

I said no to protest, but I said it wrong. Adi knew. The skin of her lips was swollen and raw. The smell of her body dripped down wrong. I was licking so much, though, I didn't care! I was an animal trying to help another animal.

"I didn't think anything bad was going to happen," Adi said slowly. "He just told me I was going to dance. I knew what dancing was. He said: 'You'll do well. You are a beautiful girl.' People have told you that, too, I know..."

She was finally speaking. I tried not to move.

"I knew who he was. He was always around, well, always leaving, always coming back. Everyone I grew up with knew him, all the parents loved him, but not this time when he came back. He was different, I don't know, talking a lot. When I went out with my friends, he kept looking only at me. One night we end up playing pool and he tells me I am someone who can go somewhere with life. He says most of my friends won't ever do anything. They'll never leave our fuck town." Adi started laughing. "Yeah, yeah, it was this kind of night. We did it, so what?"

Adi put her hand on her gut.

"Everyone's right, though. Turned out he was fucked. My parents knew I'd go, they knew something was going to happen to me, they didn't think it'd be with the man who's supposed to lead their fuck church. Whatever. Who cares. I didn't care. They all thought he was cracked when he came back that last time, completely fucky. They went: 'His brain's up his ass.' No one would talk to him but he talked to them… Yeah in the stores, he'd be watching as they took their stuff to the cash and he'd come up behind them saying: 'Mary's in your heart. There's Jesus in your blood.' I cracked up and my mother was just, 'What a shame, what a shame.' But I really couldn't give two fucks! I liked him better all fucked up. I liked him better after the whole place was pissed. They just wanted back the guy they'd helped send away with their stupid church bake sales!"

Adi was laughing hysterically.

"Yeah, he'd been to the Holy Land and he turns like some donkey ass into the devil! All they wanted was sweet home boy to come back and tell them: 'God loves you. God loves you, God loves you, God loves you.'"

Adi stood up, choking down her laughs. She started pacing quickly at the foot of the bed.

"They didn't want some guy for their church who actually knew what he was talking about."

"This is the same guy who wanted to make you pregnant?"

"My mother wants me to come back. But he has the kids. I don't care if I ever talk to her again!"

"Wait…"

Adi was staring at my wrinkled sheets. Her neck was turning red.

"On the way here we stopped at some old factory where they used to make paper. His friend met us there. They talked for a few minutes and then he told me to lie down. He pointed to the soggy floor, covered with the stuff that they turn into paper, and then he watches this guy, his friend, fuck me hard. No condom, nothing. I just lay there and waited. This pulpy crap rubbing under my shirt."

God, why does every girl have to get fucked?

"We got here in the middle of the night. He put me in a room with one other girl, kitchen down the hall. I stayed for two years. Gio came every day at the end to get my money."

"Why'd you give some guy your money?"

"Don't ask me that! Why the hell ask me that?" Adi's voice suddenly went low like a man's. "I don't like to say his name anymore. He said we'd leave after he paid. I paid so he could pay, so we could leave. He said we'd go away. We did go away, to this place in the country. He bought it for us. I did it for him twenty times a day, to make time go faster, to make it quick so we could leave."

Twenty men a day?

"I got ugly down there. White crap was coming out. Twenty times a day and some didn't use a cap. I saw my stuff coming off on their dicks, but they said it was good. They went 'unghmmmm-mmm, s'good, unggggh!'"

Adi started laughing again, jerking her hips. I saw her body flowing open, full of garbage, moving sperm.

"I scraped myself up before I left. I scraped it all out," Adi held her slip bunched up at her stomach. "But you can't change a hole! All those cocks in the hole!"

Spit was foaming at the corner of her lips. Blotches of sweat spread under her breasts in moon-shapes.

"I thought it wouldn't ever hurt me, but it hurt, it always hurt me. I think I'm wrong down there Mira. There's little pieces coming off me."

Adi's smell was stinging in my nostrils.

"Let's go away, okay, Meeeeeeera? Let's just get out of here."

"We should go to the doctor…"

"Doctor?" Adi began coughing uncontrollably and fell back on my bed. "You think I'm going to a doctor?"

I reached out and touched her shoulder. "Okay not a doctor, a nurse. My father's a doctor we could go to his nurse. She's a good nurse…"

"Your father? Your father! Your father wants to stick his hands in my pussy? Your father probably already sticks his hands in my pussy!"

Adi got up again, clutching her gut.

"You have any pot?" she asked.

I shook my head.

"Hey come on, you have pot."

I rolled over and faced the window. I don't know why I brought up my father.

"Sorry," I said quietly. "I think Lani has some."

After a few seconds, Adi slammed my door.

God, how do people get so fucked?

I wanted to cry, but nothing would come out.

He grabbed my waist and smacked the back of my ass. He started moving his knee between my wet thighs. I knew Michael wasn't watching my breasts on-screen. They were jiggling out of my nightgown. I was hot on his lap. He placed one hand on my thigh and one hand on my breast.

"Where'd Johnny-John find a treasure like you?"

I felt like laughing so hard when Michael said that. I knew he didn't like it! Michael was gay! I only did stuff with him because I knew he was smart.

"Mira is a maker," he'd said to John after he met me and watched me on tape. "You're the taker, Johnny. She's the one giving."

I felt his big knee coming up through my panties. I slid myself forward, tried to let myself melt. It felt like a glass was spinning on my chest. Michael had to be rough, otherwise he couldn't come. He yanked my wrists behind my back and never let up with the bounce of his knee.

"I swear it's relaxing. To see a young girl fucking is a totally relaxing thing."

"Shut up!" I said.

His cock was a lump. I really knew Michael was gay from the second I'd met him.

"Mira, that's good," I heard John saying. "Look up at the camera." Michael was grunting, he only took a few minutes to come. He sat there afterwards, hunched over his poor dick. Michael really made me laugh. I couldn't believe he was actually John's uncle. He was twenty-nine but he looked like an old man. I think he was going prematurely bald. Three long black wrinkles were stuck in his forehead, as if his whole life had been gouged in there.

I tried to imagine the story that John had told me about Michael, how Michael stuck his cock up John's shorts when they were kids. The reason I couldn't really see it was that I couldn't imagine Michael ever being young. I kept imagining a skinny little boy's body with his man-sized bald head. It was kind of disgusting. A little boy can't have such deep wrinkles in his forehead. Or a young person can't fuck with an old person's head.

The three of us used to sit around drinking beer after shooting and Michael would talk about all the books he used to read in university — Genet, Ginsberg, Ferlinghetti. This one time I started going off about Genet — I'd just read the book *Our Lady of the Flowers*, well, most of it, on Michael's recommendation, and by my third beer I was ranting that I didn't think it was such an "erotic masterpiece."

"Genet was the best thing that ever happened to literature, Mira,"

Michael said flatly. "He writes for people like me — 'a child-roughneck whom chance had given gold.'" Michael recited those words with his eyes closed.

John agreed, he was nodding his head vigorously, but I knew that John had never read Genet. He barely had any books. He just wrote, which was so stupid. How can you write and not read?

"Fuck you Johnny-John, you don't even know how to read!" Michael said that the second after I thought it.

I thought it was amazing that Genet actually wrote *Our Lady of the Flowers* twice. He was in prison for stealing and he wrote the entire manuscript out on the paper bags they were making. When some guard figured out what he was doing, he stole the manuscript and destroyed it. But Genet just started it all over again.

"Only fucked-up people are truly great in this world," Michael said. "Genet was a fucked-up, masturbating genius."

I told Michael that the part I liked best in *Our Lady* was when one of the characters kills his girlfriend by banging her head against the brass bed, then just looks out the window and thinks the sun is malevolent. I didn't know how Genet did that, made me follow that exact train of thought: "To love a murderer. I want to sing murder, for I love murderers!"

I kind of started an *Our Lady* game with Michael. The next time he came to John's and we were drinking, I stared at him, really seriously, and quoted from the book. "Your dead man is inside you," I said. "Mingled with your blood. He flows in your veins, oozes out through your pores, and your heart lives on him, as cemetery flowers sprout from corpses…"

"Yeah, that's good," Michael laughed. "You're smarter than I thought, Mira."

"It's the part that reminded me of you."

John looked hurt.

I rolled my eyes. "It reminds me of all of us, John. Our Lady of the Flowers is going to vomit out all our carcasses!"

Michael smirked, so I continued. I knew it was kind of dramatic: "The night, which has come on, does not bring terror. The room smells of whore. Stinks and smells fragrant. 'To escape from horror, as we have said, bury yourself in it.' "

I don't know why that passage made me and Michael crack up. I think because we both knew that John didn't really get it. I mean, that him and Michael held their dead men inside them and I was the stinky fragrant whore!

It happened a few more times. Michael quoted something about me from the book and I quoted something about him back. But then I didn't see him for a while, a few weeks, and the next time he came over, it was strange, like we'd never even had the *Our Lady* game, or the inside joke that we were both smarter than John.

If I asked John how Michael was, or what he was up to, John would get kind of mad. He'd say: "Mikey's a businessman, Mira. He can't always come over and educate you."

I missed Michael, though. Being with John was boring without him.

But Michael never came over alone again. He brought some big weird guy once who drank beer with us. I felt nervous because Michael was acting like a completely different person. He didn't say anything smart or talk about books. He just kept drinking and smoking and scratching his arms.

The only thing he said to me was: "You're always making Johnny jealous, Mira."

I didn't get why Michael and John were acting like they were friends with this guy. They were all flicking their bottle caps into the middle of the table, cheering when they hit each other.

I was pissed off that Michael was acting so stupid. As the night went on I kept waiting for him to change. But he didn't change, he just got more drunk.

It was three in the morning when he finally told John to set up the camera. "Take Joel with you, Johnny, show him how it's done." Then Michael leaned over the table to me and said: "Joel likes you. He wants to do it with you."

"Why are you so into this dirty video thing?" I asked.

Michael stared at me with his heavy pink eyes. Then he spoke very slowly: "Because I am a bum. If you do this tonight, I will not be."

That big Joel guy had thick yellow hands. I didn't know why his nails were so long. He was disgusting, disgusting, he had a thick dick, yellow hands and his dick was too hard, the smell was all off…

"Turn it off! Please! Turn it off, turn it off, turn it off!"

I made myself fall from Joel's crooked lap.

"Fuck, Johnny, she's freaking out," I heard Michael say nervously.

I looked at the screen. My vicious red face. My cunt was a monkey's ass hanging behind me.

"Turn it off! Turn it off!"

"Okay, shhh, it's okay. It's off, baby, look, it's off."

My palms were nailed to the ground. John came down quick, crouching around me. "I'm sorry, Mira, baby, I love you, come on," John's arms were tight around my shoulders. "Guys, I think you should go…"

Hurting black fluid was filling my nose. John's arms were sweltering. I wouldn't stop crying. I realized that Michael didn't give two shits about me.

But he did quote me back from *Our Lady of the Flowers*. After a few weeks, he gave John a note to give to me. His handwriting was slanted and tiny, all bunched-up like some psychotic person's scrawl.

"Her life stopped," the note read. "But around her life continued to flow. She felt as if she was going backward in time, and wild with fright at the idea of it — the rapidity of it — reaching the beginning, the Cause, she finally released a gesture that very quickly set her heart beating again."

Adi wasn't in her room when I banged on the door. I went downstairs to the change-rooms to ask the girls if they had seen her.

"Looking for your girlfriend, Meeeera?"

"You're not going to find her here, cocksucker."

"Cocksucker's looking for Crazy One?"

They knew I started living upstairs only because I was friends with Adi.

"Yeah we know why they all like you so much."

"A mouth is for eating!"

"Yeah Meera's the cockiest cocksucker!"

When I looked at them all cackling together like that, I thought they must've all come here exactly like her. Fucked and fucked and fucked in small rooms.

"Meeeera, where you going?"

I started walking towards the washrooms. Lani ran up and blocked me. She turned me around. The rest of them all grouped together and started coming towards me, going: "Cocksucker! Cocky cocksucker!"

I smelled their rancid breath and salted skins.

"You think men can stand you?"

Spit sprayed my lips.

"They can't even look at you!"

"Who gets your money, huh? How much you give him?"

I knew why they hated me.

"How much you give him, Meeeera? How much you give down-stairs?"

"I bet she sucks his crap dick so she doesn't have to give thirty."

"She'd suck a pig!"

I didn't give my money to anyone but Adi.

"What? Tongue only comes out when there's cock?"

One of the girls reached out and scratched my breast.

"Cocksucky bitch."

"Cocksucky sucks so she doesn't have to pay!"

They hated me because I wasn't like them. They hated Adi because she was more like me than like them. They hated us because we made the most cash.

They finally left me alone, crouched on the floor. The sides of my throat felt like they were touching. I heard them back in the change-rooms, laughing, getting ready.

I broke it off the night John told me he wanted us to be together forever. He said he'd felt a space open up in him the very first time he ever saw me. He told me that he always wanted to know me. "Forever, Mira." He actually said those words. It made me remember all the things I'd ever done with him when I thought I was okay, I thought I was good. Now I realized that I didn't really feel a thing. I was just doing it all to see what it was like.

I'd let him lick me for hours. John went down on me even when I was bleeding. He always wanted to be between my legs. He liked it even when I wasn't clean. He made me spread my legs, saying:

"Please, please." He wouldn't take no even if I really didn't want it. Sometimes it was the first thing he'd do when I came over. He'd get straight down on his knees, pull off my underwear and stay there for an hour, until it all just felt like repetition.

It started taking me longer and longer to get into it, to get any kind of feeling down there. Sometimes I imagined that it wasn't John's head. I pretended it was some guy I didn't know, that I was sitting at a table and some stranger was reaching under there, eating me. A few times, I even imagined that John was Ezrah.

I knew John didn't care about my fantasies. It got to the point where he was like, "I just want to be your dog, Mira."

But I didn't need a dog.

I cared for him, sure, and there were times when we had fun. John told me everything about him and Michael growing up, how their families lived down the street from each other near the slaughter house, and how they used to have these contests to see who could get closest to a dead animal. Some guy stopped once and let Michael touch the guts of a cow through the fence, John told me, excited. That was when Michael said it was barbaric and stopped eating hamburgers.

Sometimes neither of their families had heat in the house, and there were times when they couldn't wash for a few weeks because the shower was too cold. John's mom kicked him out when he was eighteen because she just wanted him to get a job. No one in either of their families had ever been to university. John lived on the street for a while after high school until Michael convinced him that he wanted to go to university. John didn't make it past the first year. He didn't like all the reading, he said. But Michael had stayed, on loans, for three-and-a-half years before it got to be too much.

"Michael hated all the bureaucracy. I mean, all the fucking

administration. He had to pay to take his exams. Total bullshit.
And then it was like karma or something, seriously. The day after
he quits school he meets the guys who're exporting our tapes at a
bar…"

"That's how you guys got into porno?" I interrupted.

"We don't call it 'porno,' Mira," John said, offended.

"What is it then?"

"It's called 'erotic entertainment.' Porno is illegal."

"It is not!" I said, laughing at him. "There's porn in every single
video store, in every single country, in every single city, on every
single screen! How the fuck is it illegal?"

John looked at me skeptically. Sometimes he could be so dumb.

John used to talk about the theatre company he wanted to open
to produce the plays that he and Michael wrote. John sometimes
let me read his stuff — it was always typed out with no breaks
between the words. I didn't understand all of it, but I sort of liked
it. John was actually funny when he wrote.

"Ilovethe/manwhotakesthebusinhisunderwear/andswears/thathe
willneverhaveawife/ortellalie." That was the name of his first play.
It was about a man who falls in love with a woman he always sees
on the bus. It turns out she's the head of the big electricity corpo-
ration that has just turned off his heat.

John could talk about his writing forever. He always held it to his
chest and asked, "You liked it, you really liked it?"

I told him I did. But I would've rather read Michael's stuff. If I
ever asked John what he wrote plays about, John wouldn't tell me.
He said that they were genius, though, because Michael was a
genius.

"Have you read them?" I asked.

John shook his head. "He's waiting for a big audience, you know?
He doesn't want to waste his time on any community theatre

shit."

"Why doesn't he ever come back to see me?"

"I think he's working on something big, you know. He'll come back soon, don't worry Mira."

I guess I stayed with John for so long because he seemed okay in the world. I mean, that he was okay considering everything he'd been through. I'd never been through any of that stuff. I didn't want to be with him, though. I knew that. Especially not the way he wanted to be with me. I remember thinking, it's okay if I do this for a little while. But after that time they filmed me with that freak Joel, I really just wanted to spit it all out. I knew Michael wasn't coming back. And I was starting to hate John's beery smell. It was always there now, as if it was my smell too.

The night we broke up I really didn't want him to go down on me again, and when he started to anyway, I pushed his head away.

"Let me, babe!" John begged. "Come on, let me eat your pussy. I love it so much, it tastes so good."

I started coughing uncontrollably. John lifted his head and got up off his knees. He went to the bathroom to get me some water. When I didn't want the water, he said, "What's the problem here, Mira?"

I was thinking: how does anything ever really end?

"What? What's wrong with you Mira?"

"I don't want to do this anymore," I said.

John's eyes sagged down. "Hey, I just want to be your dog. How many times have I told you that babe?"

"But I don't want to anymore."

John got an old joint from the table beside the bed. He started smoking it and didn't offer me any. I could tell he was angry. The room was shrinking. "You don't want to see me anymore, is that it?"

I was sitting on the edge of the bed with my back to him. I was looking around for my bra.

"Why? Huh, Mira? You tell me."

"I don't feel anything."

"Aw fuck."

"I'm sorr — "

"Don't say that. Just don't say that. After everything we've been through together. Fuck it, I don't fucking believe you."

"I'm sorry, I just —..."

"I said, don't say that!" John was pacing around in front of me. He started pulling at his chin.

"John..."

"No. Shut up. If that's what you want Mira, then just go."

"Go? Go where?"

"Goddamnit. Just go. Get out!"

"But, it's too late right now."

"So?"

"How am I going to get home?"

"I don't know. A smart girl like you will think of something."

John grabbed the sheet off the bed from behind me and wound it around himself. He was blinking wildly. "What're you worried about? Get that look off your face. C'mon, they'll think you're a whore. All men think that a woman alone at night is a whore. For fuck's sake. You gonna cry now? Stop it. Don't be a baby. Fuck. You're not a baby anymore. You're the one who wants this."

"Does the bus run all night?"

John started laughing. "You'll find a way home! Go back to your mommy and daddy. Go back to your little life."

John poked my shoulder to get me moving. I heard him exhaling hard. I was looking around on the ground for my bag.

When I finally got all my stuff together and was walking to the door, John stayed close behind me. He was making pissed-off breathing sounds. For a second I was worried he was going to push me down the stairs.

"She thinks it's all just going to end when she wants it to?" John opened the front door so hard that it banged the wall and sprayed plaster. "You finally getting the fuck out of here, huh?"

I didn't want to cry. I didn't look at John's face. I ran down the stairs and heard the door slam behind me. I stood outside on the porch for a few seconds, swallowing hard and sweating under my hair. I heard a huge crash upstairs. I thought John must've kicked in the TV.

Pounding through the streets in the middle of the night, I kept hearing his voice: "All men think that a woman alone at night is a whore."

I thought she was brave in the dark in her high heels standing there, facing the thing that wants to lodge itself inside her.

I stared at myself in the bathroom mirror. I pulled down my shirt to see the red skin on my tit where one of girls had scratched it.

"Meeeeeera…"

"Fuck!"

I rushed out of the bathroom. Adi was sitting on my bed like a man.

"You scared me! Are you okay? You were here the whole time?"

Adi stood up and spun around in a circle. Her foot was sticking out over the straps of her shoe. The top part was swollen like a little anthill.

"He's come back for me."

"Who?"

Her lips formed an O, like a dog howling down at its own stink-ing mess.

"He told me he'd come for me. He said he'd always come back. Since the very first time."

Adi started moving her hips, it was like she was dancing, but clumsy now, fucked.

"What is wrong with you? Just tell me."

"We married, it's true. I'm telling you we got married. He said: 'Do this for me. Forgive me and forgive me.' He didn't ever want me to do it with others. He said: 'I chose you.' He said: 'You'll do well.' He has a house. It's out of the city. We got married Mira! Kids!"

It looked like there was a fist about to punch Adi's face.

"He said he'd come back. He asked me to be with him. Only with him."

I stood up and walked towards her. It stopped her loose dancing. I couldn't get near, though. The air smelled sour.

"He said if I did it for him we'd live together. 'Forgive me,' he said. I danced on his lap! You know what it's like? To be with him like that?" Adi shoved her hands in her crotch. She started grind-ing. "He said, 'Forgive me. Forgive me. Do this for me.'"

"But you don't have to do what he says!"

"You don't know!" Adi whipped her hands from her pants and flattened her palms over her eyes. She stopped dancing and stood there, just kind of trembling. "Come with me now. He said you could come. There's room for you in the car. Come with us now."

I told her I couldn't. I didn't want to go. I didn't believe her.

"Look, it's okay. It's just like when we dance. Gio said you could come to his house, too. He knows who you are!"

Adi was like a little kid begging. This guy knows who I am? I was nervous to think it. Nervous to think that I knew him too.

When I didn't say more, Adi took her hands off her eyes. She stared at her feet. The hurt one wasn't moving.

"Stay here with me, Adi. Don't go, come on."

Adi looked at my shirt. She stared at the scratch. "They hurt you?"

I shook my head.

"Who hurt you?"

"No one."

"You've got to get out of here too, Meeeera."

She said my name the way the girls always did.

"Let's go." Adi reached out her hand. "Come on, let's go! Meera. Meeeera." She tried to grab for my arm. I swatted her away. She tried again.

"Are you coming or not? You coming?"

"What happened to your foot?" I was the one pleading now. "Let's go to the hospital. I'll come with you if we go to the doctor, please..."

"Shut up! Shut up! You think you know? I told you what happened. Gio's waiting for me. Car's waiting."

"Wait..."

"Fuck, I brought you here! Now I want you to leave. He said I could take you! Come, fuck it, now!"

I couldn't move. I would've blacked out if I moved. I remembered what the girls called me: "Meera the Cocksucker. Cocksucky Bitch." I knew that right then, Adi thought the same things about me.

Slowly she turned and walked out of my room, shifting her weight from the bad side to the good.

Shit, wait, don't leave me!

I went to the window and waited to see her in the lot. After a few seconds, Adi stumbled out the back door. Her arms were rigid by her sides. There was no car. No one was waiting.

God it made me sad that she was so fucked-up.

Suddenly a car drove past the club. It screeched to a stop at the side of the road. I watched Adi wave her arms and run up to it. She leaned down into the driver's window. She wasn't wearing shoes. She'd kicked off her shoes!

"Adi!" I screamed through the screen. "Wait! Don't go!"

But Adi had already run around and gotten in the passenger side. The car flashed its headlights three times up at my window.

"Stop!"

I couldn't see Adi and I couldn't see who was with her.

The things Adi told me about this guy were horrible, I knew, I really knew, but something inside me said: "You want him too." That voice in my body was saying without thinking: "He'll come back for you. Love'll be different for you."

When I followed Adi out of that bar that very first night, I thought there was no one else in the world I would've followed. Long-legged Adi with the head of a queen. But someone — Gio — he made her whimper. What kind of man makes a woman like that? She was red in the face, cringing and fleeing… What kind of man makes a woman like that? Who is the man hard enough to do that?

The smallest dicks were always the meanest. They jutted in too fast and they never slid out, just in, in, in… Big dicks were kinder. Little-dicked men wanted to kill. They made me suck their horns with my hands behind my back. Some men who came to me couldn't even fuck. They'd just sit there and sob, stroke their soft packs of veins. God, I saw so many cocks. They came to my door in one long line.

I didn't believe that I'd ever get dry. I thought: how can a woman ever get dry? But sometimes my cunt really hurt when I fucked, like a space getting carved from a heap that's too thin. But then, other times, it felt like a monster! It would get so fat, all the juices ganged up. One time, I swear, my cunt was like a buggy banging up and down on a rough, potted road, being dragged by four horses, horses pulling on my lips, horses stretching the skin from my cunt over holes, so that each time I bumped up and down it was — God! — pouring love from my holes, bumping over more holes.

I was lying on my stomach when Ezrah came into my room. The second I saw him was so fucking funny and I rolled around in my sheets like a kid.

"You're here, Ez! Come here!"

I thought for a second his lips were already kissing mine.

"Ezrah, you came! I haven't seen you for so long! I can't be mad at you now. You came, you came! Let's have fun, babeeeeee. What you want to do?"

"Are you stoned or something? Why are you talking like that?"

"Nah, No! You just look so fucking weird in here, baby. I'm used to seeing you with your arms around your mother!"

Ezrah rolled his eyes and turned back towards the door. I was laughing with my hair in my face.

"Ezrah, stop. Come on! I'm just happy you came! Come over here."

"I'm not getting on that bed with you Mira. You're fucking fucked up. I know you're stoned."

"So? It's okay. What's the problem? You're stoned too."

"What are you talking about?"

"God, I've had sex with so many people."

Ezrah wasn't standing straight. I could see his knees slowly softening under his pants.

"Ezrah, just come lie with me, darlin'."

He was stuck there, staring like he didn't know who I was.

"Ezrah we'll just talk!"

"You are fucked-up."

"So? You don't want to talk?"

"No."

"Why are you here, then?" I felt like a lunatic. There were hairs in my throat.

"I wanted to see you."

"Yeah? See me dance? Shake my big tits around the whole room?" I wanted to spit at Ezrah's scrunched-up face. His hands were in his pockets, probably touching his stinky crotch.

"You know, I'm going to tell our parents about this," he said.

"What?" Now I started laughing uncontrollably. "They don't care if you want to fuck me!"

"Stop it."

"Listen to this, Ezzy, it's my song: 'My mother and your father were lying in the grass. My mother slapped your father right on the ass! Your father told my mother she had some fine tit, my mother told your father well lick on my clit!'"

"Fuck you, Mira."

"Yeah, fuck me! You think about it so much you think it's already happened, don't you? Well, it hasn't. It hasn't. We've never fucked."

"I wouldn't fuck you if someone paid me."

Ezrah stared at my tits. I really hated him.

"I have rug burns and cigarettes stuck to my knees. Old cocks and black hairs stuck to my lips. And I am so beautiful... Every one tells me I am so beautiful..."

"Shut up!"

"You said 'I love you' with your tongue in my ear. There was sweat in a pool on the floor all around us..."

Ezrah looked down. He didn't remember.

"Why do you still have your clothes on Ezraaaaah? You're making me feel funny, babeeee. Come on, take off your clothes!"

Ezrah walked over to my bed. "Just get up," he said. "I'm not talking to you like this."

I rose up halfway and rested heavily on my elbow. Ezrah's face soared above me like an eagle. I wanted him closer. I tugged on his arm until the breath from his nose was steaming on my temples.

Put your tongue on my forehead. Your face in my face. I want to touch your tongue to my tongue...

"Let's do it."

"No."

I bit his thumb.

"Fuck! We can't do this!"

Ezrah gripped my shoulder. I moved his hand to my breast.

"No, Mira. Come home with me. You're killing me. Please... Look, I'll tell your parents you were with me the whole time, we'll just say we were together this whole time..."

I was laughing and laughing. I didn't know why I was laughing!

"Fuck, what's wrong with you, Mira?"

"Am I sexy like this?"

I lay down on my back and pushed my tits up to my lips. I heard my mouth going "Mmm, mmm, mmm, mmm." My tongue slipped out of my mouth and I licked my nipples back and forth until they were swollen, standing straight up.

"God, you're fucked-up."

"Fuck you fuck you fuck you fuck you…"

"Let's just get out of here. No one has to know."

I heard John say to Michael: "Mira'll be with anyone. She'll do anything. She spreads her ass so wide and then she fucks like a jack-rabbit."

Ezrah was begging: "This isn't for you. This isn't you. Come home with me now. No one will know."

I grabbed the lowest part of my gut. "You're making my stomach hurt, babeeeee."

Ezrah leaned down close to me, his lips were in my hair. I strained my head up, pressed my tongue on his tongue. I was kissing his tongue. Yes, yes, yes, yes…

"Stop, Mira!"

"It's so good, I don't care. Feels so good, I don't care. Take as much as I can. Stretch as wide as I can…"

"Let go of me Mira. Fuck off! Let go!"

But it doesn't matter! With you or with them. In the store, in the car, in the basement, the ground. Behind me, beside me, squeezing my tits. Laughing at how I'm still moving and fucking. My hair is all over. I'm hidden in fur.

"I just wanna be your pussy, Ezrah. I wanna curl up in your lap."

"You're disgusting. It's fucking disgusting in here."

Ezrah walked away from my bed, wiping his mouth like I was infected. "I've got to get out of here."

So go then. Go.

"Mira? Say something."

Why do your eyes look so small in the light? They're just like dull pencils. What happened to you?

"I'm going. Mira?"

Are you crying Ezrah? Is that it? Are you crying?

"I'm going. Do you hear me?"

I grunted.

"God, fuck, just say something!"

The bricks of this building are a chimney in my throat.

"Are you fucking deaf, you slut?"

"It's not worth it to speak to a fuckhead like you!" I heard myself scream.

"But..."

"But nothing! Fuck you! In fact, go fuck your mother! You think I'm ruined. I'm not."

Ezrah looked down at his feet. His eyes were blinking rapidly.

"You said you were leaving you ugly anal bastard!"

Finally, he turned. The door slammed. He left me alone.

I rolled on my stomach and buried my head under the pillow. There was a hiss in my head: careful, be careful. It worked through my head like a worm through the mud. Careful, be careful. Careful, be careful. It was some kind of warning: you'll do anything. Careful.

HALLUCINATION

There from my window in the middle of the day, walking through the parking lot away from the club, there in the middle of shining concrete, he looked like a man walking out of the desert.

I lifted the screen and stuck my head out. I started waving my arms from side to side in the air.

"You! You wait!"

I flung myself half-way out the window, put my hands on my breasts and squeezed them together.

"Come up here! Come!"

He was holding his hand over his eyes to shelter them from the sun. I unbuttoned my shirt and took off my bra. I let my tits hang out in the air. It was him, I knew, the one who saw me on my first night — that tilted dark head, the hands full of veins. I pinched my nipples between my fingers.

"Come up here! Come!"

For the very first time in my life what I wanted and what I was doing were exactly the same thing. The man that I wanted was waiting there for me, waiting for the moment when I jumped out of the window, waiting for me with peering eyes and basket arms.

"I can't wait for you anymore!" I screamed. "I can't wait to see you up here every single day!"

Gio just stood there and watched me hang out. A sluggish smile spread across his lips. His white shirt billowed behind him like a sail.

After my second shift one night when I was already undressed and ready for bed, someone started banging loudly on my door. I wasn't going to answer but the guy just kept yelling: "Open up! It's downstairs! Open up, princess! Now!"

It was the guy I hadn't seen since the day me and Adi moved in. That mean little fucker with the brushed-back hair. He was slouching in my doorway, T-shirt too tight over his stomach.

"So this is the famous Mira," he said, smirking. "Hear you're the best of the cocksuckers."

My tongue felt thick and full of sleep.

"No comment? That's the way it's gonna be?" The guy laughed and pushed past me into the room. "Now that your best friend's gone, I guess you find out how things really work around here."

I had wondered when someone was going to say something to me about living upstairs without Adi. I'd always given her my money for the month and I hadn't paid yet since she was gone.

"Thirty per cent goes to the office each time you bring a fuck to your room. I don't care how much a fuck's given you, either. You get a hundred and you bring down your thirty."

I thought it was thirty-five. Adi told me it was thirty-five. And what about the hundred-fifty for phone and laundry?

The guy started laughing through his nose. "What's the matter, you didn't know? Man, I've seen some things... We had a deal down there, sure — me and that crazy bitch go a long way back. But fuck if I knew you didn't know. She told me she was making a bit, whatever... So that crazy bitch left you high and dry, too, is that the story?" The guy scratched his red cheek and stared at my crotch. "What a girl like you's doing here anyway, I've got no idea. But the guys seem to like you and we like the guys. They're happy, so we're happy, got it? Thirty per cent and you stay as long as you like."

My breath smelled and I opened my mouth. The guy made sure I smelled his, too. The stench of us together was milky, gross.

I barely felt myself running to the bed. Cream thickened down the walls of my throat. Why'd Adi lie? She stole my tips?

The door clicked lightly. It hurt. Finally, I was crying.

It was that time of night when light wants to break but dark wants to stay. There were hundreds of bugs flapping in circles on my screen. My hands and feet were still tingling from fucking. That last guy did it so hard my cunt was pulsing like a phantom. I had to go outside and get some air.

I'd never walked around the club at night. I knew people were hiding all over, screwing in the lots and the spaces between the buildings. I knew that they looked for each other in the park at the end of the road, past the lit-up parts, in the darkness that smelled green.

I veered left and walked up a steep little hill. Old sperm was growing like spores in the grass. I passed rustling, a grunt. I walked into the forest. My eyes turned to pins through the rows of thick trees. There was someone behind me. I crouched down and rested in front of a trunk.

I knew it would happen. This was the last time.

"Working?" a voice asked.

"Yeah."

"How much?"

"Sixty."

"Suck and fuck?"

"Yeah."

The guy stuffed some crumpled-up money in my hand. I knew it wasn't enough. Sixty? This is what I'm good for? This is how I work?

The guy pulled me up. He took me jogging through trees. Leaves were ripping down all around us. I was trying to breathe, I was skipping to run. The tree trunks were gleaming with dark purple glaze.

"Here. Stop, here."

I didn't see his face. He was pushing me forward. I banged into wood. Fuck! I should've said more. His hands on my shoulders, his weight from behind. So what if Ezrah hates me? So what if Adi's gone? My teeth grazed the bark and my knees sunk in mud. The man was holding his cock at my neck. He was trying to turn me around by the chin. I could see him, I swear, from the back of my head. He was chubby, some father, a bull with a beard.

"Take it. Come on."

Oh God, this guy had the funniest dick in the world! A stubby old mushroom with a soft wilted head. He was tapping it downwards, trying to paste with it back and forth on my lips.

"Bare back," he grunted. "Gimme bare back. Please."

"Condom," I said, shutting my lips.

My neck stayed arched while the guy searched in his pockets. The sky was the colour of bruises, the feeling of him. I promised myself: this was the last time.

But the guy started getting pissed. He couldn't find a condom. He was swearing and he started pushing his naked cock into my face all over again. This time, he grabbed under my jaw. I whipped my head from side to side, but he kept smashing the mushroom into my lips.

A growl was spreading through my chest.

I was seething. Blowing. My head disappeared. I scratched my fingers down the guy's legs. I pulled at his hairs, tried to rip his flesh.

"You little cat! You scratching me up?"

The guy's pants lay in a pool at his feet. I was stuffed in the mouth and my fingers were scurrying, digging inside his thick leather slit. I picked the whole wad. Took plastic, too. Buried it under the dirt of my knees. His balls were slapping like jelly on my chin. I tensed up to keep him from going so fast. But I couldn't get tense, something made me loose. I kept feeling this strangeness blow up through my body, up from the mud, up to my throat. It made my saliva start tasting like tin. I was sucking to swallow, to keep myself breathing, his thickness, his cock, his stale white drops.

For a second I thought that someone else was there, or something behind me, around me, a swell of warm air. Something was telling me to take his body, suck out his energy — take him from him.

I heard myself moan. The guy let go of my head. My eyes flew high to the grid of the branches.

"Say fuck me, please. Say fuck me, fuck me..."

My hands held tight onto the columns of his thighs.

"Fuck me. Say it: Fuck me, fuck me..."

"Fuck me." God! Up there in the tree!

The man shot into the black of my mouth. He collapsed to his knees. "Sorry... Sorry."

I spit out his grains. I didn't say a word.

The guy stood up quickly. I watched him from the ground. I was patting down the wet mud where I'd spat. His body loomed over me, a floating head and bulbous gut. He was pulling up his pants, zipping, trying to say something.

"It's okay," I shrugged.

Light was sinking down slowly through the branches,. It turned the trees into spotty grey poles. I watched the guy walk away until his back disappeared. When I dug out his fold, I was smiling.

I couldn't tell if Gio would like it when he saw how much I wanted him. I mean, I stared at him almost every second of my dancing. I did my tricks, pumped my hips, licked my lips all for him. It's just that everything came over me so suddenly: he was why I was still at the club.

But I'd started to hear stories. The girls were always talking. "Meeera, you're crazy. You think he would like you? Gio doesn't like girls like you. Hairy big-titty girls like you!"

They saw how I waited every night for him to come in. They saw how I changed, how I hated it if they were around him. They called him "Preacher" and they said it was his job to come to the club, that he'd paid them to come to their rooms with no fucking. "Preacher just wants to talk about the family!"

They said he'd go to the edge of their beds, put his hands together and tell them to open up their legs.

"Preacher gets on his knees and starts speaking to the pussy!"

When I tried to get them to tell me exactly what he would say, they just bugged out their eyes out and started imitating him: "You thirsty, pussy? Pussy's thirsty?" They were rocking back and forth hysterically. "Why don't you come home with me, thirsty little pussy?"

Lani told me that Gio had said the Lord's Prayer to her cunt.

I knew they were all fucking with me. The man on his knees at the bottom of their beds wasn't the same one I called to from my window — the one I knew in my head I already loved. The girls were fucking with me because I loved a man they had no idea how to love.

Only Adi might have known how to love him.

She told me that Gio went down on her once in the back seat of his car. Just once and she still loved him. He hooked her legs up around his shoulders, spat on her pussy and tongued in there deep. She thought Gio wasn't the type to do a girl like that. She said he wasn't the type to get "kinky in a pussy." But that time, there he was, tonguing so hard that she couldn't even look. His face buzzed inside her, it made her want to die. The man she worshipped was suddenly doing it — suddenly, singly, worshipping her.

The first time Gio came to my room, I met him open, with my legs already spread. My see-through panties were barely a screen. Gio stared at me hard. "Do you know who I am?"

I nodded. I knew. It was like Adi threw him to me.

"When did you first know that we were going to do this?" Gio asked.

"Right now," I lied.

I wanted him to take me any way he wanted.

Gio kneeled down at the end of my bed. I thought he was smirking at the fabric of my panties, because my hair came through its tiny holes. His eyes looked metallic.

"This is the way we must begin," he said.

I heard Gio letting out breaths through his nose. I propped myself up and stared at him. Was he really going to pray to my pussy?

Gio grabbed my ankles and started stroking lightly. He was murmuring something. I couldn't hear what it was vibrating inside his throat. Then he licked his lips and slid in towards me. A drone on cement.

I was waiting to be touched. Beating through my panties, I let out a groan. I couldn't take more. I wanted his mouth. I wanted his body instead of mine.

"Wait, you. Just wait."

Gio gripped my thighs and launched himself forward. His lips pushed against the tissue of my panties. He licked once up and down with his whole entire face. God just that once, pressing on my slit, he got me to the point where I was already gone. He finally moved my panties to one side. My black space opened up and his breath poured inside me. He stared at me there. I was too swollen to care.

Breathing from my cunt, talking from my cunt, I was bulging forth from hairy lips. It's terrifying if you look it in the eyes.

Gio used his knuckles, dipping into my wetness to stretch me and rub me. He pinched my lips with his rough-tipped thumbs. He stretched me even wider. I wanted his tongue. All I wanted was his face. He was pulling and stretching and pulling and stretching, he could've bit down and I would've spurted come. I was going to come, my breathing was fast, I was gonna come out, I was just about to come...

Suddenly Gio slithered up over my belly. His face dripped with sweat, like someone already running. He took his shirt off and leaned on one hand. His chest was one huge smooth rock of hide. He unzipped his pants. He yanked down my panties. His cock was so big it hung over my breasts.

Adi's been here, I thought. She's been where I am.

Gio was like the king of the forest, the beast who had right lording over his bitch! I was anxious, all ready and I grabbed for his cock, but the beast took my hands and stuck them onto his back. I held onto the curve where his muscles started bucking. I had to suck in my breath. Gio didn't take time. He kneed my legs open and pushed himself up. Plowing through my thickness, my blackness, my wetness, I felt my head roll over to the side. I shut my eyes and just let the juice gush. My cunt was like the shape of a boat where wood gets squeezed from two shuddering sides. The force of his thrusts carried shocks through my chest. I wanted his come, right at the back of me, right at the end. With Gio on top of me, moving and fucking, I felt myself being forced through the bed. He was fucking so hard that my body hit earth.

"I always knew," I said between his thrusts. "I always knew me and you were going to do this."

Gio pulled out and spurted on the rise of my gut. One short sound fell out of his throat.

He stared at his stuff on my belly for a very long time. Then he wiped me off with the sheet. He left the bed and went into the bathroom. I heard the shower running.

I flapped around on the bed still feeling his cock in my cunt. I was like a fish needing water, more salt in her gills!

And I still hadn't recovered when he came out of the bathroom. He was fully dressed. I was flat on my back. Gio leaned down to kiss me. "I'll be back," he said.

I didn't make him pay.

It was like he'd just given me something. Something I wanted that I couldn't say out loud. When he was in me, I didn't want to come. I just wanted him to stick me, over and over, because with each of his thrusts, my pussy got tighter. My pussy got hotter and stronger so it could hold him in there. Each second we were fucking, a voice in my head breathed: "I want you, I want you, I know who you are."

I felt that the very first time that we fucked. Gio was someone I already loved. So what is love but already loving?

God, why do I love him more than he loves me? Why do I love his body so much more than he loves mine? It's like he is the woman and I am the man. He's the indifferent one and I'm the one ravishing!

I know the way the flesh feels on his stomach. I know the way his back rounds at the top. I know the width of his neck and the mark on his forehead, the mark that I think is from praying on the ground. Forehead to ground, flat feet to huge hands. The skin around his centre is animal-thick. I mean it: his skin is like animal skin, stretched out so smooth, you keep wanting to touch it. He's like a bear, a great walking bear. You just can't stop staring and wanting to be closer. Where everyone else has regular skin, Gio's skin is magnetic, shining. Something comes out from his face that's alive, some kind of ray that pierces through my weak protection.

Gio came back for me seven days later. Fucking bastard, it took seven long days! This time it was noon and I was just getting up. He was wearing a grey suit jacket, which was strange because it was still so hot out even though it was September. He sat beside me on the edge of the bed and started tickling my ribs with his fingertips. I had to choke back my laughs. Then he did the same thing up near my throat. That made me yell, louder than I meant to. My head was lifting off the bed and slamming back down and Gio began tickling me even harder from throat to waist, throat to waist, until the whole bed was moving and I was spinning. I squeezed my eyes and let myself go…

"Shhh, Mira! Stop breathing so heavily."

My eyes opened up. Stop laughing? Stop breathing? Gio's lips were pressed together. He was staring at my neck. He thought he was looking at my face, but he wasn't. I knew that look from other guys. The glazed eyes that meant: I want to be with someone I don't feel guilty about right now.

"Hey, why're you wearing that jacket?" I asked loudly. "Where were you? Where are you coming from?"

Gio nodded his head back and forth so slowly that the room got gloomy. He wasn't going to tell me where he had been. I knew things were better when I just waited for whatever he wanted to do to me.

But Gio kept sitting there vacantly, like I'd ruined the moment or something. I felt like calling him "Preacher" to see what he'd do.

"Is something wrong?" I asked. "Did something just happen?"

All of a sudden, Gio took off his jacket and arranged himself over my body. His thighs locked like walls at my sides. He scooped his hands under my neck and brought me up to the big lump in his crotch. The smell of sweat charged the creases in his pants. I wanted to rub my face in there, burrow.

"You're hungry, yes?" Gio asked. "Tell me you're hungry."

I was mute. Hungry.

"You want to put it in your mouth?"

Yes. Up and down, up and down like a fool!

"Why do you like putting things in your mouth?"

I don't know. Just give it to me!

As my mouth opened, Gio's zipper came down. He let out his cock. I couldn't look at his face. His cock was the only thing I could look at: the thickening root, the slit like an eye. His cock was the part that already loved me.

Put it in my mouth, gimme, gimme, gimme, please…

"If you don't speak, we'll do it like this then."

Holding the back of my head, Gio shifted towards my face. He placed his hard flesh on the groove of my tongue. I was stunned. I got hot. I dropped into his cradling. I was sucking his body in gulps down my throat. I wanted to swallow to see how we fit. A suctioning clasp. Forever. No key.

With my mouth on his cock and his cock in my mouth, I didn't remember any other man I'd ever been with. No other man had ever been inside me. I was a bud, sprouting fresh from the mud.

It was daytime when I went back to the park. I walked to the top of the hill, up a set of wooden stairs. I hadn't realized that there was a clear way up — that what looked like a forest at night was just a bunch of crooked trees.

I could see the club down at the end of the street: the silver door where the men came in and the brick part at the back where all of us lived. The buildings of the city were packed together in the distance. The sky hung above them like a heavy white sheet.

I noticed that some of the girls were sitting around in a circle on the grass. They were passing a bottle, waving me over. They all looked the same with their dark hair and dark clothes. Julie was there, she stood up to call me. She was the only one I'd ever thought was okay. She was the only one I'd ever seen talking to Adi.

"Come, Meera!" Julie shouted.

For a second I thought they might all start being nicer to me. As I got closer, though, I saw that some of the girls had their heads in their hands. They were smoking and shoving their cigarette butts into the grass. I sat down a bit outside their circle. Julie passed me the bottle. I took a sip.

"What is it?" I coughed. It was fizzy and sour.

Some of the girls started laughing. "All of us are drinking it, Meera."

"Yeah it's to clean out your mouth!"

"It's for cocksuckers, Meeeera!"

Julie reached out and pulled me into the circle. She was stronger than I thought. Her arms were so thin, all those girls were so thin. I realized that some of her makeup was smudged. She'd been crying, smoking? I never really liked how these girls danced, it was too jerky and rude, not like Adi. But suddenly, it was fucked-up, they reminded me of her... Marisa and Lani reached across the circle and tugged me roughly into the middle.

"Hey you guys, don't."

That one sip made me feel sick. It was prickling up my throat. I put my head on the ground. The butt of a cigarette smoked in my face.

"Cocksucker doesn't like it?"

"Come on, you guys, Adi liked her!" Julie cried.

This time it was different. I mean this time it was different that they were calling me cocksucker. Adi was gone. She had taken my money. I was with her man and I couldn't help it.

"Look at her! She likes it."

A finger on my thigh, then a finger on my ass. I felt two in my stomach, three on my breast.

"Stop it, you guys, Adi liked her, come on!"

The rest of the girls rolled me onto my back. Two took my shoulders and two took my feet. Liquid was splashing. Five sour fingers. I heard the girls laughing: "Money's for home! You send money home!"

There was a push in my gut. I felt it and I didn't.

"She's dead," Julie whispered to me through the rotten air.

I saw all of us spinning above our bodies, hands in a circle, stretched wing to wing. Deep in my head I heard something snapping, one tiny wishbone broke in each ear.

She's not dead! I knew Adi wasn't dead.

She'd called me from the road a few days ago. "Meeeera, I'm cooooold," she'd moaned too loudly. "I'm on the highway. It's cold. We're going to his house. I haven't seen them in soooo looooong. He's shaving. You drink coffee? I'm drinking coffee… He wants to impress them? Fuck, crap it's cooooold! My foot hurts, Meeera. I don't know if I'll make it all the way up that stupid stone hill. He doesn't love me. I don't want to make it, I know he doesn't love me…"

Adi started to cough. I was trying to say: "No, he does, he does, he does."

"It's okay. No, I know. He doesn't want to do it with me anymore. It's too cold. My foot hurts. He's not going to come back."

My heart started beating really fast. I wanted to tell her about me and Gio, but I couldn't. It was as if there was no room in her body for more pain.

"Men suck your breasts when you got milk in them," Adi said gruffly before she hung up.

The girls poured the last drops of liquor on my face. I squeezed my eyes shut. I couldn't tell what was the truth and what wasn't. I didn't believe what anyone said.

"Meera, money goes home!"

"Cocksucker, home!"

I thought that Adi was more like the other girls than like me. There on the ground, in the centre of meanness, I knew the biggest difference between us. I knew that the girls would never go home. They wouldn't leave here like I would. Because some girls can do things like fucking for cash and they're never the same, they can never go home. But some girls can do things and always escape — they fuck up their bodies but always feel new. This is a thin and dangerous line.

It was early in the morning the next time Gio came. "Morning has broken," he said, at the bottom of my bed. He had a strange look. His eyelids were flickering. God, why did I want to be with him so badly? Why did I wish that he would just climb into bed and get naked with me? Why is it so good to lie naked with someone you love?

It sounded like Gio was humming for a second. He was some old man letting it come out through his nose. I didn't move. A tight grin held his face. I smiled too — but mine was all teeth with the cheeks aching hot. He made me like that.

"I'll see you then, Mira…"

"You're leaving? Wait!"

Gio walked to the door and told me to meet him in the parking lot in five minutes or he would leave. I didn't have time to dress in anything good. I didn't put on any makeup and I didn't brush my hair.

When I ran out back, Gio was standing beside a smallish white car. His hair was matted right above his forehead. He opened the passenger door for me. I tried to smile but I blushed instead.

The seats were covered with burlap and the car smelled like gas. It had a bit of trouble starting, but once we got out onto the highway, everything seemed all right. We were driving east, away from the city. Both of us were quiet for a long time. I kept trying to think of something to say, but nothing seemed right. And I wanted to ask him about Adi, too...

"Where is your family, Mira?"

A low scraping noise suddenly started running with the engine. I looked behind us. Gio accelerated.

"What's that?" I asked.

"Don't you speak with them?"

"Who?"

"Your mother, your father."

"Not really," I said.

I wasn't going to talk about my family with him. I didn't even want to think about my family with him. My family was nothing inside this car. Even my Ezrah shit was forgotten.

"What does your father do?"

"Why are you asking me?"

"Why don't you answer?"

"He's a doctor."

"A rich doctor?"

"No. He has enough."

I bet his next question would be: "Why are you doing this?" Everyone would ask that next. I bet Gio thought he knew everything about me — where I was from, how I'd grown up. I wish I'd just said to him: "No family here."

"And the brothers?"

"I don't have brothers."

"No brothers? Poor father."

I snorted.

"And Mother?"

"She teaches."

"Teaches what?"

"Religion."

"Religion." Gio started coughing. "What kind of religion?"

"I don't know, all kinds."

"Your mother teaches 'all kinds' of religion? You think there's 'all kinds'?"

I was glad he was hacking. Why did he want to know about my family? That my mother taught kids the Hebrew alphabet? I wasn't going to tell him I was Jewish.

"We have a long way to go," Gio said abruptly. "Why don't you sleep now."

Fine.

I stared out the window. The clouds were all withered. I felt myself fading, even though I didn't want to. My chin kept dropping onto my chest.

Then, it was strange, my eyes popped open. I mean, I thought I was dreaming but my eyes were wide open. It was me and Gio still driving on the highway, but in the distance I saw all these people running towards the car. There were hundreds of them, coming closer, throwing rocks at us, plates at us, garbage, rats... The highway got narrower and the people smashed their faces on the glass.

They were flat-lipped, screaming: "Let us in!"

I was trying to scream too: "Keep driving! Keep driving!" But nothing came out. We must've run over something. There was a sudden dragging sound. I turned and I saw there was blood on the road, square blood printed in a line behind the tires. Air bubbles started popping in my chest. I knew there was someone dying underneath us. "God, get away!" I was trying to wake up. "Get away! Get away!"

"Shhh!" Gio was gripping my shoulder.

"Where are we going?"

"Calm down. You're okay."

Gio took his hand off me and slowly rubbed his face and chin. I was trying to focus on him. For a second, he reminded me of John. The way all men's cheeks are rough and black.

"I sent the children out a few months ago," he said. "I knew it was going to get worse in the city."

"What?"

"The house where my kids are."

"But what's getting worse?"

All of a sudden I thought of the girls waking up at the club. Me and Adi fucking in our rooms…

"I don't have a wife," Gio said, glancing over. "I have a woman at the house who takes care of them when I'm not there."

I knew it: Adi was never his wife.

I realized that Gio had draped a coat around me while I was sleeping. The coat had slipped down to my waist. My nipples were hard, I felt them through my shirt. Gio kept turning his head to look at my tits. I stared straight ahead and slit my eyes. I wanted to make myself feel even more. His staring was making heat flash through my body.

"I had to remove my children from the city where filth is

worshipped. Where girls show their true colours before they reach twelve. Their mother left them alone in this waste-land."

Gio spoke calmly. I didn't think I wanted to know about his kids. I just wanted these feelings inside my breasts to continue. I want-ed my liquid to spurt on the seat. I was with a man who had come to my bed twice. A man I didn't make pay. The man who fucked Adi up? A man who muttered on his knees to girls' pussies?

He'd never love you Meera! He doesn't like girls like you!

The trees beside the road were getting thicker, all the trunks stacked in the same darkened lines.

"She was a little like you, their mother."

Fuck, I didn't know why I said I was in love!

"Relax Mira," Gio said softly.

I closed my eyes. We drove along in silence.

I started thinking about Ezrah. It was his birthday soon, the tenth of October. I thought I might call him. I just wanted him to know, I guess, that I remembered. But I was too embarrassed to call or too mad to call, maybe too gone to call. I didn't even know which one I was more. Why couldn't Ezrah like me no matter what I did? What if I cleaned shit from the streets for a living? What if I was legless, leprous, contagious? Why couldn't he love me just because I'm here? Just because I'm here, is that a reason he shouldn't love me? I said it over and over, every which way: why don't you love me with come on my hands? Why don't you love me legs spread for the crowd?

"I don't love you," Ezrah would say, "because this isn't you."

Yeah? Who am I? You tell me who I am.

"The Mira I knew when I was a kid, the Mira I want when I'm feeling alone."

So what's the problem?

"There's shit on your knees, it's all over your knees."

Fuck you, there's no shit on my knees.

"Only I can see it. You can't see shit."

You see, I knew he would say something like that.

"Jism is not invisible, Mira."

Go fuck yourself Ezrah! And fuck your jism-flecked birthday!

"Who do you pray to?"

Gio's voice startled me.

"What? Nobody."

"That's not true."

"What do you mean? It is."

"It is not."

"Okay," I said slowly. My eardrums were beating. "I've never thought about it, then."

"While you were asleep, you were crying for God."

"I was not!"

"Yes you were. You were crying, 'God, God!'" Gio imitated my voice. He seemed to be getting more comfortable with me or something.

I stared at the road. The road never changed. "Look, I'm not religious," I said.

Gio laughed. "Do you know why we pray?"

I nodded my head.

"Yes or no?"

"No."

Gio rolled down the window to let in some air. It started whistling over our heads.

"We pray," he said slowly, "to believe in the flesh of Jesus Christ. The real man, with real blood. Did you know this, hmmm?"

I felt weird that he'd just said "Jesus Christ." The heat in my body had all gone away.

"You don't know?"

"No."

Gio shifted around on his seat. It was like he was trying to itch inside his back. "When we kneel before the priest," he said, "the body of Jesus is put in our mouths. We say: *Hoc est corpus meum.* You know what that means? Come, say it with me."

I thought he was joking.

"*Hoc est corpus meum.* Come, say: *Hoc est corpus meum.*"

"No."

"Mira."

Gio was so stern that I laughed. "Okay, okay. *Hoc est corpus meum.*"

"Good. 'This is my body.' Say it…"

"This is my body."

I looked down at my chest. My nipples were huge again.

"And when the priest holds up the goblet of wine, he says: *Hic est calix sanguinis mei.* Say it…"

"*Hic est calix sanguinis?*"

"*Mei…*"

"*Mei.*"

"This is my blood. Say it…"

"This is my blood."

My gut rumbled.

" 'He who shall not eat my flesh and he who shall not drink my blood has not life in him.' John 6, 53."

Gio looked at me and nodded, as if I knew what he was saying. But I'd never heard this kind of thing before. I didn't know anything about Jesus or John.

"We pray," Gio continued, "because Jesus was a real man. He had a real body and real blood. We pray because Jesus showed us his body, his unclothed body pierced with nails, so that we could look at his wounds and remember our own."

Gio stretched his huge fingers over the steering wheel. Jesus was crucified, that much I knew.

"The very first time I met the mother of my children," Gio said, looking over at me briefly, "she wanted to kiss me, she wanted to 'do it.' But I held back. I didn't want to be an animal with her. She just gripped my neck and was going to sink her teeth in..."

Instinctively I reached out and touched Gio's neck, where soft baby hairs flattened down on the skin.

"I couldn't stand that she was doing the same thing to all those other animals."

We turned off onto a smaller highway. Gio stopped talking. He let me work out the kinks in his neck. I felt him start to relax in my grip. When I was in high school, some girl told me that Jesus was killed by the Jews.

Suddenly Gio twitched and something cracked in his neck. My hand flew off and stuck to my lap.

Gio took out a handkerchief from his pocket. He pressed it to his open mouth. It looked like he licked something out with his tongue.

"Do you know why God told the prophet Hosea to marry a whore, Mira?"

"What?"

"Why would God tell Hosea to marry a whore? Would many men want to marry a whore?"

"I don't know."

Gio swallowed loudly. "They'd be disgusted. Why?"

Disgusted? A whore?

"God forced Hosea to marry a whore," Gio continued. "Because being with a woman who'd slept with so many was the only way to show him the real way to love."

Am I loveable? Am I easy to love?

"You think this is easy for a man, Mira?" Gio's voice rose. " 'For she is not my wife,' said Hosea, 'neither am I her husband. Let her put her Whoredom out of her sight, lest I strip her naked, and set her as in the day that she was born, and make her as a wilderness, and set her like dry land, and slay her with thirst...' "

"But the man is usually the one who makes a woman promiscuous!" I blurted out.

Gio kept talking as if I hadn't even spoken. "Hosea was obeying God by taking the whore as his wife," he said. "And I was obeying by touching that one — her black hair, her long limbs. I was meant to love her, forgive her and shield her from even more exposure. I saw her staring at me in the club with her golden eyes. The devil's eyes. I saw her wanting what I had, Mira, wanting what was in me. But she wanted too much. She was the most beautiful one around and she wanted to stay that way."

I imagined Adi and Gio twisted around each other. Gio and Adi on the seats of this car.

"The beautiful ones always want to be seen. The beautiful ones want to see themselves and watch what their bodies can do. Turning dancing into sex is too easy for a young woman."

"But they do it so well because of that!" I said.

Gio squinted at the road. I think maybe I'd just made him mad. "I need a girl to dance only for me. I want her breasts and her heart for myself, not sticking out for all men to see. 'I will discover her lewdness in the sight of her lovers,' said Hosea. 'And none shall deliver her out of mine hand.' "

Gio was gripping the steering wheel so hard now that his knuckles had turned white.

"I had to keep that one at home. I had to make her pregnant. I had her feed me and clothe me and I would feed her and clothe her. The very first night we were together she said: 'I know you are a good man.'"

"It's true," I said softly. But I meant: it's true, girls are insatiable.

"Her eyes were painted dark. Her hips were always shaking. When I felt her skin I could never get enough. Her skin smelled like sex. Her thighs smelled like sex. She had sex peeling off every part of her. God gave me this whore so I could cry, so I could get down on my knees at her thighs and pray: 'You are my wife. You'll only ever need me.'

"I took her in my car. She was laughing and looking at herself, rubbing and shaking herself. I thought this was the one God had sent me, but she was acting like a beast with the light pouring out of her. I had mercy on her, Mira, I went down on her to hold her, to stop her from moving in circles. She was moving in circles all over my tongue. I kept making her cry. I kept obeying her there."

Gio licked his lips. I squeezed in my cunt, I was wet.

"Did you know that Hosea had to pay another man to get his wife back? He loved her and still she kept on being a whore. He loved her and still she didn't want to be with him forever. Forever, how a man is to be with his wife…"

I realized the car was veering onto the shoulder. We'd slowed down too quickly and dust was rising all around us. Gio got out of the car and slammed the door hard. He walked to my side and started knocking on the window. His eyelids were peeled back, his white eyes were bulging. He was struggling to open my door, but I was holding it tight.

"Get out. Open up!"

I didn't know why I was holding the door. I thought the pain that he felt was the same pain I felt.

Gio stormed around to the back of the car and opened the trunk.

His shirt was soaking under the arms. All of a sudden, I let the door swing. I wanted to be open.

"So, get out then," said Gio. He was back in front of me now, breathing hard.

I didn't feel my legs move.

"Get out I said!"

It got cold inside my forehead. Why was he yelling?

"I want to give you this, Mira," Gio said.

I thought my face was showing I was afraid.

"Just get out of the bloody car!"

A pearly white dress unfolded from his fist. It was swinging between us. Still I couldn't move. Gio's hand came down for my wrist. The second he touched me, I flew up, I don't know how.

"That's better, Mira."

I was standing there in front of him. Gio lifted my shirt up over my head. His thick fingers reached behind me and unhooked my bra.

"I don't know why you always wear this thing. I like it better when your breasts hang loose."

Gio watched my nipples get hard in the air, then he slid the dress onto me.

"Now you look beautiful."

The dress was shiny, too tight at my sides. And I was itchy suddenly, as if there were hairs at my nipples.

"Take off your pants."

I stood there for a second, then I started to turn away from him. I was slow, so slow that he probably couldn't see I was moving. I was aiming to put my hands on the roof of the car...

Gio grabbed me roughly and spun me around. He unzipped my pants, jerked them down in one tug. The door handle was stuck between my legs. It was making me pulse. My cunt was all wet. I felt him staring at the tilt of my ass. I pushed it out a little. I think it was the only thing on me that could move. I think I'd been waiting all day to fuck him! I flattened my breasts down hard on the window. The silky dress made me slide on the glass. I heard Gio's zipper and a car racing by. Then he lifted the skirt of the dress. He felt between my legs for my soaking hot mound. Gio ripped my panties down to my knees. I was stuck there dripping with them stretched and tied around me. Then the head of his cock hit the line of my ass. I wanted to tell him to just put it inside me, split me open, right open, fuck me right now! I bent my knees down to try and tell him, just do it, but Gio leaned his massive chest down, a big slab on top of me, pinning my wrists. He breathed in my ear, "You're the next. You're the next."

I got hotter and wetter. "Next, you're the next." I wanted to reach out and spread it, spread my ass wide, but my hands were locked tight: "God please, Gio please…"

"You're the next, you're the next."

All of a sudden I thought that he was going to be my husband and I was going to be his wife. I'd be a good wife, a great wife, a hot wife! I'd be the woman he'd been waiting for forever! The one he'd come home to every single day! I'd love him at home and suck him at home, bathe him and feed him and fill him at home…

Gio stuck his tongue in my ear. "Mira, Mira, you're the next."

I thought he was in love with me. I felt we were in love. He's in love, he's in love and I'm in love, too!

But it was only for a second, both of us like that.

Love is so strange it can hardly bear more. It's a nightmare vine, a plant with a face, wood with the veins ripping through, squirting come. Love is one second inside these dark folds…

"Fuck me, please fuck me!"

I want your come!

"Mira you've got a hungry little pussy."

I want to be like Adi when she's dancing.

"Mira little pussy, little cub, little whore."

I want to be the next whore that you save.

We were struggling and humping. My fingers stretched out. Gio turned me around by the chin. He pushed his tongue in and out of my mouth. I was a sponge. I'd take anything from him. I thought I was going to come in a second, just from us kissing, just from the wind, just from my clit banging into the car. Clenching my cunt, I squeezed and let go. The rushing, the fucking, my ass got all split. My legs were all locked. The sides of the road extended forever. Then his cock was inside me. His cock pushed so hard. His cock went up through my cunt like a rock. There was nothing between us. This was how I loved. Hot on his stone, oiling it down, I was holding it inside me, squeezing it inside me. My cunt loved his cock. I wasn't letting him go, he was fucking me harder so I could take more. His cock pushed in all the way to my clit and my clit flowered open, a bulb from inside. I choked, I came, I heard it in my throat, his tongue through my lips, his cock in my cunt, I came and I came! His pulsing fat dick pushed the come into my cunt.

God, wait, don't stop!

Gio's cock left me.

I collapsed inside the car. I was wet on the seat. I pushed away the burlap and scrunched it at my feet. I was going to cry. I wanted to cry. Because I wanted to go back to right where we just were! Where my cunt was so strong that I was showing it off! And I wanted to do it again and again, just like a leech sucking blood from the bone. But I wouldn't cry. I hid my eye in my shoulder. A hard pain shot through my body and lodged itself inside me. Gio got back into the car carrying a pillow from the trunk. He wedged the thing between my face and the window. He said, "Sleep for a bit now. Go back to sleep."

I didn't want to be asleep again. The feeling of fucking was too strong inside me.

But when I closed my eyes for a second, the lids stuck together. And I saw a bed, this big white bed with two people in it. They were sleeping together in the middle of a room that had huge stone walls arching up to a point. I didn't want to feel Gio's head in my head. "Now I lay you down to sleep..." I didn't want him awake while I was asleep! "I pray the Lord your soul to keep..." Something started happening low in my legs. It felt good for a second, light for a second: I was running through air so thick that my hips took me up. Ten feet aboveground, as if I was flying and running and swimming all at once... "If you die before you wake..." Then something inside my stomach fell down. I looked between my legs. A tiny gross head was dangling out of me. It had short curly hairs and sour white lips...

"Mira!"

Gio was standing outside the car shaking me. I was holding my stomach. I thought I was bleeding. I shoved both my hands down there: thick, fuck, I got it.

"Rise and shine," Gio said.

We were at the bottom of a driveway that curved up a small hill. Gio's palm was in front of my face. He was holding the handkerchief that he'd pushed to his face in the car. It was filled with little cream-coloured pills. It almost looked like they were home-made. White dust was coming off them.

"Take one."

"What is it?"

"Take it."

"I got my period."

"For that."

"Is it good?"

Gio nodded. I didn't move.

He took one of the pills and wedged his fingers between my lips. I opened my mouth and it fell on my tongue. It tasted moldy and came apart fast. I just wanted to run and get to a bathroom, but Gio was staring between my legs. There were blotches of brown in the creases of cream. It was making me want to vomit, his staring. My gut felt like it was being scalped.

"I've got to go clean up," I said. My period always started really strong, blood all over my legs for a day.

"There's the river out back. Do it there. Wash that too."

He was serious? I was bleeding and he wouldn't let me into his house?

Gio leaned his head down inside the car. Above his lip were clear drops of sweat. I thought for a second he was going to kiss me, but instead he gripped me by the arm and lifted me out of the car. My toes were clenched. I knew I was leaking.

"Come on," Gio said. He was irritated now.

The ground was made of sharp white stones. Just a little way down from the driveway was a still brown pond in the middle of a creek. It looked like a place where people washed pots or scrubbed their hair.

"Go," Gio said as we walked towards the water. "Go on, get in there."

I tried to look at him, because at that second I wanted him to keep me. I said it exactly like that in my head. Keep me. Keep me. Keep me...

"Will you come in with me?" I asked.

Gio's eyes roamed up and down my legs. He stared at my stain on the crotch of the dress where I held it in a clump. He looked revolted.

Keep me. Please. I wanted to shout it: keep me! Keep me! I wanted him to be with me the way he was with Adi. How did she love
him? How many loves can we have in this world? How many loves
are there to be filled?

"Go in there, Mira." Gio poked my ass.

To stop myself from crying, I walked in tiny steps. To stop myself
from crying, I held the dress between my legs. I was thinking
maybe we could stay here a while. I'd hang out with his kids. I
didn't want to be in this freezing, this cold! I wanted to lie
between sheets with Gio beside me.

Please keep me, please keep me, please keep me, please…

"Go on! Get in there!"

I was right at the edge where water was lapping. I've lost it, I
thought. I fucked up. He'll never feel that way about me.

I moved bit by bit down into the pool that had turned black and
blue as I got closer. My thighs, then my stomach, then my breasts
disappeared. Long weeds were floating on the surface of the water.
I scrubbed the dress between my fists and let it flare out big like
a blossom.

So this is my body. *Hoc est corpus meum.*

Red smoke rose from between my thighs and settled like scum on
the surface of the pond. I felt like laughing for a second — so this
is my blood! *Hix est calixus sanguina* from my pussy…

When I looked up, I saw that Gio had walked to the edge of the
water. His hands were lifted as high as his heart. Trees waved
around his head in a circle. He was watching me, patting the air
in downward strokes. I imagined Gio's hands were touching my
shoulders, pushing me down to where everything was ice.
Breathing fast through my nose, skin turning to scales, I ducked
underneath the freezing cold plane. Gio's hands pushed me down.

I thought he was in there with me. Adi are you down here too? I was hearing my name the way the girls always said: Mmeeerraa! Meeeeera! His mouth on our mouths, our cheeks split like fish… Meeeera started to fizz from the ground to the top of my throat.

"Meeeeeeeerrrrrra!"

I shot up for breath. Gio's body, chest bare, was coming towards me. I was dizzy from gasping, dizzy from swallowing, I was walking sideways in short jerky steps. Who was this man who was walking in towards me?

"Fuck, what did you give me? I feel dizzy. I'm stoned…"

Gio looked weirdly different in the water. His hair was tighter to his skull, his skull seemed thinner than his neck. The bones above his cheeks protruded, temples beating…

"I had sex the first time with an illusion," he said.

This is what you're confessing to me?

I couldn't help grinning as I glided towards Gio. My body suddenly felt good, cold-sucked in the dress.

"I stared at a girl in a pornographic magazine. There was no hair on her vagina."

Gio placed his fingers at the corners of my lips, he was trying to close my cracked-open grin. "And I did not feel anything upon emission," he said gravely.

"Nothing? No, I know you felt something…"

I reached through the water and unzipped Gio's soaking pants. I found his dick, all waxy and limp. My grip kept slipping off its head. I liked it when a cock was soft and I was the one who made it hard.

"The first time it happened, I didn't feel a thing. I just saw what came out of me, what stuck to the sheets. I wasn't happy with myself Mira, do you understand this? I got down on the floor, put my forehead to wood and prayed that my body was not real like

114

the others."

Gio braced himself on my shoulder as I pulled on his cock underneath the pond.

"God said the emission could be erased by burning. He said that inside my body was fire."

"Yeah, you're hot," I slurred, giggling. "That's why I know you. You're perfect. You're hot. What'd you give me? This pill. Hey, is it good?"

"It's good," Gio said, his eyes at the sky.

His cock was getting so thick in my grip. I rubbed faster and faster, looking up too. Then I saw the house up behind him. A house with a spire. The house was a church? No the house was a nunnery! A man with the nuns! I started laughing hysterically. "You live with some nuns?"

"No, Mira. Men live in a monastery."

"Where? Were you there? Was I there?"

"In Palestine, yes. I studied for three years."

Gio took my hand off his dick, lifted it up out of the water and spread it flatly on his chest. His heart felt like some kind of frog: cold, deliberate, rasping.

"When I was at the monastery, Mira, I had only one occupation: meditation on God's words. I let my mouth speak whatever it wanted, because I knew all my words were bound to their root in Heaven..."

Gio lifted my arms and started twirling me around.

"Lift up your arms, Mira. High, higher. Don't forget your legs, lift them too! Lift your legs, stand on your head! In happiness too there are heavy animals!"

I was dancing and splashing, the pond was a swamp! The swamp was a river! Outside Palestine runs the river Jordan!

The sky started turning purply red. I saw rain in the clouds before rain came down, vibrating holes from the tiniest grids. I knew rain would squirt through those clouds and pour out, dissolve like glass splinters into our skin…

"Let's get out of the water!" I splashed Gio's chest. "Let's go and lie down in the stone room and fuck!"

But Gio didn't budge. I stopped my wet dance.

"I thought I had reached perfection," he said coldly. "Do you know what it feels like to think you've reached perfection? In the presence of the others, I said it out loud, I wasn't afraid. 'Is there a person on earth capable of teaching me anything?' I asked. 'Is there some kind of spiritual achievement which I have not attained?'"

My feet sank into the clay of the creek. I felt a big clot of my blood release.

"Of course, the monks didn't want me to say these things. I had reached way above them and they didn't want me to speak." Gloom settled over Gio's face. His eyebrows were thick, all in one line. "Then one day while I was praying," he said. "A shadow came near me. It sat on my collar. I thought it was a crow."

I put my hands on Gio's thick waist.

"I was told to leave," Gio said harshly. "The monks said: 'Go. You must leave now. Go.'"

I wanted to pull us in towards the shore, but I couldn't feel my feet. Everything was numb.

Suddenly Gio got down on his knees. His chin bobbed just over the surface of the water.

"I left on the Sunday of the first week of Lent. All the monks came to see me off. They kissed me three times. They were glad I was leaving. I was glad I was leaving, too, because I was moving ahead of them. And the crow was not gone. My crow got upset. It started to spit up long, twisted worms. Its beak was coming apart in my ear." Gio closed his eyes. His bottom lip had turned blue. "I left my home, my school of three years, with only some bread, some figs and some water. I crossed the river Jordan. I did not touch the food because the bird had started branching out in my body. 'You have stained the coat of your flesh,' it told me. 'You have torn the first garment the creator wove for you. Therefore you are naked, soiled and ashamed.'"

Gio looked sick. I stroked his wet cheeks. "Please, let's go in..."

"What does it mean, Mira, when people say that truth is all over the world?"

"We need to get out of here, you're going to freeze…"

Gio opened his eyes and glared at me hard. "It means that Truth is driven out of one place after another, and must wander on and on and on."

That's it. I was hit. Punched through my stoned daze. The sequence was clear: I met a man, then I met a man, then I met a girl and I followed her to him… I did what she did, she left and I left with him. Now I remembered, I knew how I was who I was! Struck dumb! Open ears! I know how I know! Truth is driven out of one place after another and wanders on and on and on…

"I walked through the desert for many days," Gio's bottom lip made small undulations in the water. "And I slept at night with only the sand beneath me. I had already walked for twenty days when I stopped and turned towards the east for my midday prayers. Suddenly, without removing my eyes from the sky, I saw on my right the shadow of a human. At first I was sure it was the devil that had come to take me, but then I saw there really was some kind of person, walking alone...

"It was a woman, Mira, and she was naked. Her skin was black. I thought she was scorched by the heat of the sun.

"I got up off my knees and started running in her direction.

"But when the woman saw I was approaching, she began to run away. I followed her quickly, as quickly as I could, but when I got near, she just ran faster. When I thought I was close enough for her to hear me, I began to yell: 'Why are you running away from me? Why are you running? I'm a man. I'm a sinner! Wait for me, God! Servant of God! Whoever you are, in the name of God, for whose sake you live like this in the desert, wait for me. Please, unworthy as I am, I beg you, stop and grant me a prayer and a blessing for the sake of God who despises no one! Speak to me, God, for God's sake, speak!"

Gio jumped up off his knees and the water exploded. I started screaming, loud. My ear-holes were prickling, the shrieks of a crow, she was running away, the skin of the woman, her hair caked like mud, she was running away from him, running away!

"It's okay, Mira, we're getting out now, shhhh..."

Gio was holding my hand and leading me out of the water. I couldn't stop shaking. She was running away...

We lay side by side in a small patch of sand, our clothes and our skin covered with grains. I stuck my hands between my legs.

"I should have known you'd be upset." Gio said, stroking my face.

"I can't feel my feet."

"Nothing is wrong."

Gio found his handkerchief of pills under his clothes. He took two out and put them on his tongue. I nodded no, I didn't want any, but his thick fingers split open my lips.

"You are safe in the desert with me."

Gio laid a white tablet in the middle of my tongue. Shivering, I didn't feel myself swallow. I tried to bury my feet underneath the sand. I think both of us were starting to get really stoned. I was just really stoned. That's all I was.

"Why am I here?" I felt those words repeat a few times.

"You're here with me, Mira, because there are sounds in your body. Sounds that come from under your skin."

He stroked my shoulder. Rough palms, sharp feathers.

"Listen."

"Wait…"

"Listen."

"Wait…"

Okay… There are sounds. These kind of shrieky little mewls.

"There are sounds that you make when I'm around. I've called all the other girls, but they don't respond. You knew who I was and my vibrations were received. You saw what I wanted and your want responded. Blessed is the girl who can save needy souls."

"Amen," I said.

Amen, I said? That felt so funny I wanted to say it again…

"Yes, you hear the requests of unworthy men and you pray to the Lord for the whole world and them that their wandering through the desert should not be without fruit. You are the one who can do this, Mira. I know you are the one, the only one."

Gio pulled me tightly to his chest. It was cold and still wet. I licked his black nipple.

"Gio," I whispered, through the buzzing and the mewls. "Will you… Will you… Marry me?"

He released me from his grip, suddenly blank.

Oh.

Shit.

What'd I just say?

It was like some big discharge had just rattled all the sounds. Suddenly I couldn't look at him either. I had to get up from the maggoty sand. I had to take off this fucking dress! I jumped up and quickly went back towards the water, tearing the dress up over my head.

Blessed is the girl who can save needy souls. Amen. Amen! Fresh blood down my thighs. Amen. Amen!

Let him watch me.

Now let us squint...

Something hazy was hovering over the pond. All those dots from the clouds were dripping through the air! Huge in the air, they were fighting around me, or the mewling had died and it turned into air. My ears were starting to feel full of the haze. My heavy red cunt was full of the haze.

All of a sudden I felt ready for something big. Fuck becoming a stupid wife! I was ready for every kind of game in the world! I wanted to look at pictures with Gio, how I used to do it with Ezrah and the guys. Naked men and big girls, kissing each other, licking each other, swallowing and disappearing inside each other. Feeling that restlessness spread through my body, itching and rushing fluorescent white waves. I had sex the first time with an illusion, Gio had said. I had sex the first time with illusions and illusions! Ezrah and the guys had huddled around me, I was down like a blob on my stomach and back. The magazine was spread so we could do it how they did. Those guys made the rules until someone's finger pushed in me. Until I felt how big I was there and how small the finger was, how nervous it was!

I didn't turn around at the edge of the water. I knew Gio was still sitting there, watching my naked ass, my parted legs. I stroked my waist up and down for him.

This time the water was strangely lukewarm. The foaming edge of it filled between my toes. I started going forward. My foot didn't sink. I was skimming it forward: my foot did not sink! The arches of my feet were like the sails of a boat and underneath my soles was warm air. This water, my body, I think I know how I did it. My legs swelled naturally into balloons. Steady in my pelvis was a helicopter pulse. I was a body made up of water. All of my blood was softer than water. I could walk on this, fly on this, skim or dissolve. Wait, I know how I did it! Air on top of liquid is liquid slicing air. Blood is the way to lightness flight. This helicopter haze. It lifted me up! I walked forward on the water. Wait, I know how I did it! And I knew I could do it a million times more! This was real, not a dream, everyone could do this. Lift up and move with the pulse in your ass, spray from your heart, play some up and down blood. Everyone, everyone, everyone should feel this! The haze that allows us to walk on water. It's real, not a dream, this was real, not a dream…

"Daddy! Daddy!"

I spun and I fell. Shit! Two little bodies were running down the hill, heading straight for Gio's legs. Gio scooped his girl in the middle of her dash, and threw her high up into the air. Shrieking, she had the same skinny legs as Adi. The boy raised his arms, he wanted up, too, but Gio wouldn't stop twirling his girl.

I was crouched under the water now, up to my chest. My heart was making sounds like the frog. The boy saw me first. A boy with a little paunch already. He was staring at me with dark eyes and dark lips.

"Is that the new one? Is she going to stay?"

Gio put his girl down and frowned at his son.

The girl started jumping up and down and pointing at me. "Is she gonna come out of the water? Daddy, tell us that story with the woman from the water!"

"Not right now, sweetie, no."

"Please Daddy! Tell us that one. How did you tell it? Please, tell us, please!"

Gio cupped his palm under the girl's chin. "Like water, love clings when you hold it loosely. Like water, love goes when you grip it too hard."

The girl clapped her hands. "Like water, loves clings when you hold it too loosely. Like water, loves goes when you grip it too hard!"

"Yes, that's it."

The girl was laughing, looking up at her father. Then she smashed her smile in his thigh.

"Is she going to stay?" The boy asked again.

"No. She's too wet to come inside now."

Gio's daughter was staring at me strangely. She put her finger in her mouth and started wiggling it back and forth. I tried to smile. I'll stay. Yes I'll stay. I wanted to say it so they could hear me. The words came through my lips in bubbles: "I'll stay. I'll stay."

Gio put his arm around the girl's shoulders and they started walking up the hill. The boy followed, but he was looking back at me. Like water, love clings when you hold it loosely. Like water, love goes when you grip it too hard. But truth wanders on and on and on... I watched them walk up towards the house. The boy picked up stones from the driveway and threw them back at me. I'll stay! Okay? I'll stay!

Gio put his arms around both his children and ushered them inside the front door of the house.

I walked out of the water. Freezing, I got my clothes from the car. I shoved heavy bunches of tissue in my underwear. Then I crashed down in our small patch of sand. The sun hit my throat. Why was I alone? Why was I alone now, when the three of them were together?

All of a sudden I wanted some voice to tell me that what I was doing was wrong.

My feelings for Gio were all wrong, all wrong. Even my feelings about Adi were all wrong. I thought I needed some voice to punish me for fucking, for fucking without thinking, for fucking in a chain.

I thought I'd just let the devil have my body. I thought I'd let the devil in the shape of a crow first spread me open and then sew me shut. I am serious. I'm serious. I was dreaming of confession. I wanted to be clear.

"Listen, Ezrah — everyone's path is from pure to disgusting. There's some moment that wrenches our nice things away. There's only a few years in our lives when our mothers will keep cleaning us. There's only a few years before our mothers put us down. But we still want to get picked up and thrown in the air! Our mothers say no and our fathers say no. They say: 'Children have to walk and learn to clean themselves.' So how do we learn to clean ourselves? How can we love each other when we are so filthy?

"Yeah, I clean shit from the streets for a living. I clean piles of shit so you don't have to see them!

"Ezrah, this is about a secret. You still loved me, I'm telling you, when I was fifteen, when I was out every night with Michael and John. When I was silent, constipated, stuffed up with rags. You still loved me, even though you didn't know it. You were always so smart. You never got in trouble. You told your parents lies when you drank with your friends, when you drove their car blasted out of your brain. They still bought you your own one when you were eighteen, they still paid for your school, they still thought you were good. Ezrah, you've always been so smooth. Your lies and my lies should be the same. But I guess what happens when we grow up is that some of us swelter and pour forth the goods and some of us freeze and dive into the cracks.

"You know, I saw this couple the other day walking hand-in-hand on the street and I knew exactly how they had sex. It's my talent, Ezrah, I have X-ray vision. I can see how people fuck. And I saw that these two fucked so well, even in hatred, because she was the lock and he was the key. It sounds stupid, I know, but it really works like that! Cunts and cocks have to fit — if they don't then they're fucked. You know how people fuck when they're in love? One person gives up their sex for the other. They say: you have my pussy, you take my clit. And: you take my balls, you take my cock. One lover volunteers to be neutered if the other lover can be doubled with sex — full of the power of the pussy and the dick!

"Yeah, real lovers are magnets, not attracted to shit. Shit makes you tired. Shit really smells. Fucking's for parasites who feed off shit! I clean the shit, you understand, Ezrah? It's a compulsion I have. I'm confessing my compulsion to deal with shit. The shit in the well, at the bottom of the well, the shit in the pool and the shit in the lake…

"Listen to me. What I'm saying is this: fear is my realm. I'm waiting for fear. Because before anyone comes in, from the moment I'm wet, fear's stooped beside me, it's inside my gut. So this is what I do, this is what I play with. When I'm with a strange man, I'm waiting for fear. It feels really good to meet this fear."

I heard Gio's steps crackling down the path. The sun was almost down. I had used up all of the tissues from the car and buried red wads of it under the sand. I waited until his body cast a shadow over mine.

"We have to go now," he said.

"But I thought..."

"Yes?"

"I thought we could stay here."

"No. Not here."

"Why?"

Gio leaned down and stroked my head. The ends of my hair were still wet, all sticking together. Gio took my hand and helped me stand up. He walked over to his car. He looked like a soldier motioning for me to follow. I stood there and looked up toward the house.

"Why can't we stay?" I didn't understand.

Gio had already started the car. I ran over and got in beside him.

"Close the door, Mira."

The muscles on the backs of my legs started spasming. "Why aren't we staying?"

I shut the car door. We pulled out of the driveway. I thought I saw the kids waving from the porch.

At first we drove down a narrow mud path. Branches scraped the sides of the windows. We turned left onto an empty paved street before we got back, too soon, to the highway. I didn't want it to be over yet.

"Is everything okay?" I asked.

Gio didn't answer.

"Well, was it good to see your children?"

"Yes. It is always good to see one's children."

I opened my window to get some fresh air. Why the fuck was he acting like everything was okay?

"So their mother was your wife, right?"

"No. She was my lover for a very long time."

"Adi?"

125

"Roll up your window, please."

"Is this why Adi left? She couldn't take how you spoke?"

Gio cleared his throat. I leaned my head into the glass.

"When did you become a whore, Mira?"

"A whore?"

"Yes."

"I don't think of it like that."

"You take off your clothes, show men how you move. You open for money. This is a whore, am I right?"

Gio smiled hugely. It was the very first time I had seen all his teeth. His front bottom two had childhood ridges. They were shining like bluish pieces of snow.

"All great whores become pure," Gio said. "Even the foam on her lips becomes pure."

The air in the car was blowing, unbearable.

"Mira, do you know how a whore becomes pure?"

"I don't know." She swallows buckets of come? She fucks up the ass? I wanted to say that and burst out! Ha ha ha ha!

"I beg you Mira, in the name of God, for whose sake you have wasted your flesh in this way, you can't hide who you are or where you came from, when and how you came to be in this place. If it weren't pleasing to God to reveal you and what you have achieved, He would not have allowed anyone to see you and He would not have given me the great chance to meet you."

"Meet me? Gio! But we've fucked! We just fucked on the way here at the side of the road!"

Gio started to drive insanely fast. "Mary wandered in the desert for thirty years to become pure. She was only twelve-years-old when she left her parents to travel with a man. And she kept on travelling, alone, city after city, to let all the other men take her the same way. Mary did this out of insatiable desire. She wanted to wallow in the trough, Mira. That, to her, was life."

"I had sex the first time with a scumbag named John," I said. "He and his uncle used to film me wallowing, too…"

"One day, when Mary was walking at night, she saw a great crowd of men: Egyptians and Libyans going down to the sea. She stopped one of them and asked where they were going. 'We are all going to Jerusalem for the exaltation of the Holy Cross,' they told her. 'Do you think they would take me, if I wanted to go?' Mary asked. 'Anyone who has the fare can go,' the man replied. 'Indeed Brother,' Mary smiled, 'I have neither the fare nor any food, but I will go and get into one of the ships and they will take me even if they do not want to. I have a body that will serve as both fare and food for me!' Mary wanted to go, you see Mira, so that she might experience more lovers, so that crowds of men could watch her."

"Once, a carload of guys drove by me. They were hooting at me, late at night on the street. All men think that a woman walking alone at night is a whore."

"Yes," Gio murmured.

"They said they were going to Cherry Beach. They had beer and they asked me if I wanted to come. There was something about the smell of the night, I don't know, or their heads hanging out that made me get in the car. They just watched me and drove, no one said a word. At the beach, they made a fire. We were drinking. I was laughing when I took off all my clothes. I danced around their circle and they clapped and hooted. I didn't really want to like it so much but they knew. I knew. It's a nightmare right now: cocks stuffed in my holes, from behind and the front. I was crouched open in the sand. I spread my lips wide. When I turned, they were laughing. 'She can do us all,' they said. I was drenched in their sweat. Threads of sperm on my thighs."

"Mira."

I was silent.

"Do you know how to repent?"

A grunt.

"Tell me how you will repent."

"Fuck till I'm sore."

Gio ground his teeth together. "You must learn how to repent," he said.

I let out a grunt and a snort.

"Think about where your mouth has been. Think about where your hands have been, your open legs. Don't you know what you have absorbed? You have sucked men's sinning right up inside you. These guys have sex with you. They watch you. They watch how you move. They do not think good thoughts about you, Mira."

"That's not true! They do. I know they do."

"No. The whore is the woman he beats out of his body."

All of a sudden I remembered: Ezrah in his car with me when I first told him what I was doing. Ezrah in the car with me outside the temple, slamming the door. When he left me alone I pulled the shawl I was wearing up over my head and I covered my face. I slid my hand under my dress, into my underwear and I lifted my leg. I stuck a finger inside my ass. The first time I ever felt there. A dark tight unloved inside.

This was how I atoned for our sins.

"I knew it from the very first time you came near me, Mira. You are an open furnace, able to feel anything. I'm telling you this for a reason."

My throat constricted. I put my hands over my eyes.

"If you repent for your sins, God will take you back. God promised the whore His undying love. God sings to the whore His

128

saddest love song. 'And I will betroth you to me forever,' He sings. 'I will betroth you to me in faithfulness.' I am telling you Mira, that there are whores who have been wandering in the desert for thirty years. They the ones who truly know the Lord…"

I took my hands from my eyes and looked out the window. God was not watching. Watching as I fucked.

We were back on the busy part of the highway now, speeding by gas stops, bright cubes selling food.

"After having sex with as many men as she could, Mary finally made it to Jerusalem for the Festival of the Cross." Gio glanced over at me as he spoke. "But she found that the church would not let her in. She tried to go in with the swell of the crowd, but as soon as she set foot at the threshold of the church, something repelled her, Mira, some kind of force," Gio paused. He kept checking on me. "Mary suffered this way five or six times, watching all the other people enter easily, until eventually she gave up and stood in a corner of the court. Suddenly, a feeling spread through her…" Gio paused again. He was enunciating every word. "Mary thought it was the consciousness of her uncontrollable lust that prevented her from going inside the church. She wept and grieved and beat her breast. It was her heart coming open that made her beat more. 'Help me,' she prayed to the Mother of God. 'It is not a man that I need anymore!'"

I was leaking through the tissues now, sitting tall in blood on his white car seat.

"Mary needed the Mother of God. She got down on her knees and this is what she prayed: 'Virgin and Lady who gave birth to the Word, I see that it is not suitable or decent for me, defiled as I am, to look upon you, you who always kept your body and soul clean. It would be right for you in your purity to reject and loathe my impurity…' " Gio was making his voice go high and girlish.

" 'But help me, please, for I am alone. Receive my confession, woman to woman, and let me enter the church. Do not deprive me of the sight of that most precious wood upon which was fixed God-made-man whom you carried and bore as a Virgin! Oh lady, let the doors be open to me so that I may adore the divine cross! To learn the ways He showed us how to die to the world — how to die in our heads, not in our bodies; how to let ourselves die by burying ourselves in horror, to die to the world but to rise and live again. I beg you, Mother, from whom God became flesh, to guarantee my promise and I will never again defile my flesh by immersing myself in horrifying lusts.' "

I let the world come inside the car. I let my vagina melt into the seat. I let my feet descend to the highway. Through sudden holes in the floor of the car, I was starting hot sparks with my soles on concrete.

"I can feel every cock that has ever been inside me," I said.

There was silence for a time. Buildings grew up ahead.

"When she promised to never again defile herself," Gio said, "Mary was let into the church."

"Are we almost there?"

"Mary was ready to be led to salvation. The voice of the Mother of God came to her and said: 'Cross the river Jordan and there you will find rest.' "

"I think I'm going to be sick. Can we pull over for a second?"

"When I met her, Mira, she'd already been wandering for years. A naked woman who had not eaten for years."

I wanted to be home. I was swallowing, fighting the vomit back down. I closed my eyes to shut up my throat. Right then, I knew: Adi was really dead.

Gio's whole body was shaking strangely. I wanted to curl far away from him.

"The only thing I thought to ask the whore was if she thought of human contact here in this desert, that thing for which she used to have such great need. And this is what Mary told me: 'As for the thoughts that would push me into Whoredom again, when such thoughts grow in my body, I fling myself to the ground and flood the earth with my weeping.'"

Gio's voice as Mary's was creepy, full of strain.

" 'And I hope that she will stand by me again and again, she who has been my protector, my saviour. I do not get up from the ground until her most sweet light shines around me and drives away the thoughts raging in me. I am nourished now by incorruptible food, and I cover my shoulders with hope — for woman does not live by bread alone. All who have no clothing will be clothed in stone, we who have discarded the outer covering of our sins…'"

"Stop talking like her! Stop saying what she said!"

Gio stared at me so hard that I put my hands over my eyes again. "Well, do you understand?"

I nodded my head back and forth. Yes, no, yes, no. Get me out of this fucking white car. Get me to a toilet quick.

"Jesus said that we must bring forth what is within us or else it will destroy us. Take your hands off your face, Mira, say that to me."

"But I've welcomed every cock, I'm telling you! Every dirty, hot and cursed!"

"We must bring forth what is inside us…"

I felt myself smiling with shame.

"We must bring forth what is inside us, Mira…"

"We must bring forth what is inside us, Mira…" I repeated.

"Or else it will destroy us."

"Or else it will destroy us.

I dropped my hands. We were almost back in the city. What was inside me was good, hot and cursed. What's good, hot and cursed is indestructible, isn't it?

I was a girl who could walk on the water!

Stopped at some lights with my eyes flashing red, I heard Gio say: "Jesus does not desire the death of sinners. He guards them with his loving kindness, waiting for them to be converted. Do you understand?"

"I do."

"Because Hosea loves his whore. No matter what she's done."

We pulled into the parking lot at the back of the club. I wanted to run up to my room alone, but Gio turned off the engine. I just wanted to be in my room by myself. I couldn't take anymore tonight. I didn't want to hear another thing.

"I'll come in with you," Gio said.

"It wouldn't be good right now," I said quickly.

"What?"

"You coming in."

"Why?"

"I'm fucking tired."

"Look at me."

I couldn't. My head was a bowl that would crack if it moved. Gio was staring right inside me, through my cheek, through the skin. "I'll just be going to sleep, Mira. I'll be leaving very early in the morning."

"I don't think it's a good idea."

Gio grabbed my shoulder.

"I'm not going to feel well, please." I knew Gio wanted me to look at him the way he was looking at me. "I'm going to be upset." My voice was choking up. "I won't feel good, okay? I know I won't feel good."

Slowly I looked over at Gio. His nose was so broad, his lips so were large, skin magnetic, eyes spreading, I couldn't believe it. Every animal was appearing inside him — black bear, soft lion, white dove, demon crow…

"Breathe, Mira."

Gio had his hand on my forehead. His thumb was pressing the curve between my eyebrows. I closed my eyes for a second. It was red behind my lids.

"When you're with me, we'll sleep and you'll be fine."

Somewhere I knew that the whole of me wasn't in it, somewhere I knew that the whole of me wasn't there. It's just that my doubts were strapped on like bombs.

"Where is she?" I asked tightly.

Gio was silent. He pressed his thumb deeper in me. God, really, where was Adi?

"Keep your eyes closed," he said.

The lids were burning hot.

"What do you see?"

"Red. I see red."

A low buzzing ring filled up my ears.

"Where's Adi? Tell me where she is."

"I don't know where your friend Adi is."

"But did she leave with you?"

"Close your eyes."

Red leaves exploded from a tree in all directions.

"No, Mira," Gio said softly. "She did not leave with me. I haven't seen her for weeks."

"I can't say no when you're right here."

I let heat glow from inside my face. Adi and Gio — their names roamed up and down. Something he was doing made my body relax. Something he was doing told me she was okay.

But when Gio suddenly took his hand off my forehead, a coldness flooded to the bottom of my gut.

"I want to know where she is!" I opened up my sticky eyes.

I looked straight up into Adi's old room. A shadow moved away.

"Mira, believe me, I don't know where the girl is."

I knew what that girl was doing up there.

I got out of the car. I walked ahead of Gio to the back door. My hands were holding between my legs. He put his hand too lightly on my back.

When did you become a whore? he'd said.

All girls are whores! I should've spat back.

The air smelled like piss. I really thought I was going to be sick. I wished he would just leave me alone now. Up the stairs, the vomit got higher in my throat. The rough grey walls were dripping with filth. I opened my door, ran to the bed and threw myself down on my stomach. I stuffed sheets in my mouth so I wouldn't gag, wouldn't puke.

After a few minutes, I felt the mattress sink down under his weight. Gio didn't touch me. He'd taken off his clothes. I felt him reaching over the bed, looking for something in his coat. Then he rolled over and tapped me on the face. Another pill was in his hand.

"Take it. It will help you sleep."

"No."

"Trust me. It's good for your dreams."

Gio set the pill down on my pillow. I didn't want any more of that shit. I watched him arrange a pillow over his eyes. Then he pulled the sheets up tight around his neck so that all I could see were his lips.

"Go to sleep," Gio murmured. "Trust me. Take it. Go to sleep."

I wanted to bleed the rest of my period over the bed, all over the sheets, deep down into the springs of the mattress. I wanted everyone to know: Mira was here.

I put the pill between my teeth. I bit it in half. It was definitely yeast.

I thought I might get that feeling again...

But back in this craphole I was stuck to the bed, staring at a man: a lump with a mouth. I felt like some dumb adoring mother who couldn't stop ogling her only creation.

Why'd you tell me all those things? Why didn't you let me come into your house? Because I let so many people inside me? Do I have to beat my own breasts? Do I have to run away?

I thought there was only one way for me to get out of this place. I needed the things that were running inside me to just stop for a second. I needed to see what was making the horrors come true. What made me become a girl full of stress? What made me decide to be with some man for my very first time and then never say a word?

I saw John again. He actually came to the club one night with Michael. I froze like a fool when I saw the two of them because I thought somehow they knew I was there and they wanted me back. But after watching them for a while, I realized that Michael was sick. He was bony and pale, his clothes were practically falling off him. I thought: he has AIDS. John looked like some kind of gorilla beside him.

They were drinking beer and chain-smoking. John was over-excited, eyeing the girls.

"So it's fifty a song, big boys," I said, leaning on their table.

I swear, John's jaw dropped when he saw it was me. I started laughing hysterically at the expression on his face. I couldn't help it. He looked like someone had just kicked him in the balls! Ha ha ha ha ha ha ha ha ha ha! John was frowning and pushing his chin to his throat.

Michael started laughing too. "You still watch the Mira tapes every night, don't you Johnny?"

It was like John didn't really want to see me in the flesh. I had on my pink cut-off T-shirt, the one that was so short you could see the bottom of my tits. I was standing above him with my hands on my hips.

Ha ha ha ha ha ha ha ha ha ha ha ha!

Michael kept looking back and forth between me and John. His eyes were alive, but it was horrible.

"What's going on with you?" I asked.

Michael started coughing so hard he had to put out his cigarette. "Nothing," he finally got out. "What makes you think there's anything going on?"

"You look like shit," I said. Then quickly added, "Sorry."

"No, Mira, it's you that looks like shit." John was angry. He lit another cigarette.

"Shut the fuck up, Johnny," Michael snapped. "Mira looks hot. You look a fuck of a lot hotter as a lady, Mirabella."

"Just get rid of those tapes already, will you?" I spat at John, feeling half-embarassed, half-proud from what Michael had just said. "I'm not your fucking eternal release."

John nodded. Michael smiled at me calmly. Lights flashed over his face, never stopping. "Our Lady," he said, suddenly sitting up tall. "If I were to put on a play in which women had roles, I would insist that these roles be performed by adolescent boys and I would so inform the audience by means of a placard, which would remain nailed to the right or left of the sets throughout the performance."

"Amen," I said.

As I looked at Michael, I felt my face multiplying smiles. I wanted to touch the side of his head. I leaned down towards him and put my lips on his cheek. "It's okay," I whispered.

Michael nodded vigorously, he was chewing his bottom lip.

"It's really okay," I said again. "None of it hurt."

I turned to John before I left, but he wouldn't look at me. He was sucking so hard on his cigarette that all the paper had wrinkled. I rolled my eyes at Michael and whispered: "Tell Divine I say goodbye, okay Darling?" Then I spun on my heels and went straight over to a table of guys who gave me a bill to start dancing.

The next time I looked over, the two of them were gone.

It occurred to me that maybe Gio saw in me what John and Michael had seen. It occurred to me that Ezrah saw something completely different. I pitied Ezrah sometimes. I ached for Gio mostly. I was dumb because of John and I was smart because of Michael.

Why was I stuck in this big loop of men?

It felt like there was some tiny person standing inside me, right down between my navel and my cunt. Someone three inches high, who took me at twelve or who took me at twenty, who took others like me at twelve and at twenty. Someone inside of us, yelling and whispering: "Here! I am here! Here! I am here!" And that tiny person with the squeezed-together face made us spread our legs wider to see what was really going on. Was she the one who was making us do all these things? Or was it us that wanted to be forever excited? I needed to know, was it her or me? Or was it him or him or him or him? When I let a man in, it was all repetition and the person inside me, she just spoke louder, in beats and in slaps: "Here! I am here! Here! I am here!" Until I knew that she was so far up in me that she couldn't be prodded out by a finger or a cock. The person inside me was too sensitive for that. She flinched and melted every time she was touched and she shrieked in my ears every time she was not. God, I was really watching myself now…

Gio snored loudly. He rolled over onto his back.

I felt like I was spiraling down into the bed. I had to push up and lean my head against the wall. The room became a box and we turned into miniatures. I heard my breaths. They didn't sound right, they were short little gasps coming hot through my nose. I moved an inch closer. I wanted to touch Gio, something, start squeezing, squeezing quiet. I wanted to see if I could move the sheet from his chin, slowly, without waking him. I thought if I squeezed some part of his body, I wouldn't feel like falling, rolling off the edge…

Fuck it! Fuck! I wish you were my slave! I'd strap your head like a belt to my cunt. I'd open your lips and pull out your tongue, your slick purple tongue would be wiggling to lick me. I'd force you to swallow my sticky soft moss.

I was running my hands up the shroud of Gio's body. I stopped over his cock. I wanted to make it rise under the sheet. I wanted it to spurt, just from my thoughts.

My slave has the most beautiful cock in the world. His cock goes inside my mouth like a spoon. Feed me, feed me like a slave, feed me. Feed your sister, your daughter, your mother, your lover…

I got up on top of Gio, straddling his body, my knees around his sides, my hands near his face. My palms moved closer. I couldn't hold back. It sounded like there was straw in his throat. My hands were going to stick on his lips…

"Wake up!"

Gio tried to roll over. "What? What are you doing?"

I was sitting on his legs, staining his knees. "I have to leave here," I said.

"This is what you're dreaming?"

"I can't be here anymore. I don't want to do this another second."

Gio put his head back down on the pillow. He shifted his legs so I'd get off him.

Wait until I say it: I understand. God marries whores. That's what you told me. Listen, please listen. You can't say no. Wake up! Let's leave. If I say it out loud, if I say it again, the answer will be yes. I know the answer will be yes. Yes, yes, yes we'll go, yes.

"I want to…"

"What?" Gio grunted, almost asleep again.

"Go with you."

"Mmmm."

"To your house."

"Not now."

"But…"

"What?"

"I want to stop doing this."

The sheet was back up at Gio's chin. His eyelids were purple. "Everything's going to be fine, Mira. You're dreaming. Go to sleep."

But I'm awake! Wide awake. I just told you everything! You thought you wanted to be with me and now you don't? Nothing is fine! Why didn't you let me into your house?

Gio was snoring. I started to get itchy. My body felt like it was breaking out into hives.

Tell me what the fuck happened to Adi! How could you have loved her and still called her a whore?

It was Adi who told me all girls are whores. But those who stay whores die.

There were pains in my cunt. I couldn't stay another second. I felt sore, red and salty. Just like her.

I was on the verge of waking him again, but he'd be even madder. Like water, love slips… I was scared of the sounds going round in my head. A pulse in my head was as loud as lips smacking.

I realized I was pressing my palm down, pressing down on his breathing. There was a small gurgling noise. I was going to get on his cock while he slept, with my knees round his sides. My ditch and my moss. Stop breathing so hard! Stop breathing so hard! I just wanted to make his cock grow. The neck of a bird come to life between my legs…

Fuck you, Gio! What are you good for? Your cock is all smashed like shit underneath me. I could kill you. Kill you! I want you hard. I want it so that you die being hard.

My palms started buzzing. My eyes were blinking back. All ten of my fingers were asleep to the wrists. That's how I got off him. I ran to the bathroom with fingers clenched shut. I got in the shower, hands purple, turning yellow. I forced them out of their tightly bunched fists. My cunt was itching. I was spraying it clean. I was thinking about his daughter. What about his daughter? Did his boy hate me too? Well that little girl will get her daddy back, because I didn't do anything! I really didn't do anything to him! You'll get your daddy back! I wanted to sing it, screaming. You'll get your daddy back! But you'll never know your mother!

When I came back into in the bedroom, Gio was perfectly still under the blood-marked sheet. From above it looked like birth and at eye level, death. An iron-like smell filled up the room. I hated him and loved him, it was too close to take.

I grabbed Gio's grey suit jacket from the chair. It was so big it hung down to my knees. I felt for his car keys and clasped them tight. I got my money and some clothes. I heard his gentle panting.

I shut the door softly. I ran down the hallway. It was three in the morning. Leaving, I'm leaving! I was banging it out on all the girls' doors. Leaving, I'm leaving! Leaving, I'm leaving! I love you even if you don't love me!

VIGOUR

I had a dream about Adi. She was standing in a kitchen. She was bigger or rounder than I remembered. She was leaning head-first into the oven when suddenly flames leapt out onto her skirt. I was sitting at the table and I rushed to try and help her, but there was a yellow crescent field curving around her waist. I couldn't put my arms through it. I had to stand there and watch as Adi bent in the oven more. Her hair and her shins and her arms caught on fire. She was all yellow, right down to her feet. Then I heard hissing at the bottom of the oven.

I think this is what happened: Adi was in the parking lot, running to that man. She got into his car with her eyes still swollen and I bet she laid her head in his lap. I bet she felt his cock swelling on her neck. With the back of her skull touching the wheel, I bet that's when she said: "Shine your lights up at Mira."

As they drove off, I bet Adi let her tongue loosen and made noises for him to take her. I bet the man parked behind a factory down the street, unzipped himself and pushed the head of his dick onto the wet of her lips. He had a thick, dull piece of him that wanted to be free. I bet Adi was murmuring, "I, I, I," because she thought that whenever she had a cock in her mouth. "I and I and I and I..."

Maybe Adi was happy she was sucking the mottled or black or purple-pink dick. Maybe she rolled her head on his thighs, not wanting his thing to come out for a second, as if cock was the air she needed to breathe. I bet she pumped her hips up and let the guy touch her. She slit her eyes and saw what she wanted: the guy above her holding her hair, his finger in her pussy and his cock in her mouth.

I bet the guy marked her with shots of his come. When the drops hit her cheeks, I bet Adi screamed, squeezed the base of his prick and I bet the guy yelled: "Easy, hey, easy there, give me a chance to recover."

I bet Adi felt the man's finger like a nail in her pussy when her pussy felt huge, huger than the car.

Adi had never cried after men but this one, the very last one, made her wail.

"Oh Jesus," the guy was probably saying, "What did I do? Jesus, what'd I do?"

But I bet by then Adi was sobbing uncontrollably, because it finally made sense to her: the first and the last. My first and my last are by nature the hardest. I can't stop my ending, I can't stop my failing, I can't stop washing my body in tears. Adi was holding her face, crying and swooning. But the guy couldn't know what was happening, really.

I bet he just slid the cash over on the seat and said: "Hey, hey darling! Shhh, take your cash. I gave you a nice tip. You sure earned it, darling. You want to go back now?"

I bet the guy wanted to shake Adi's shoulders when she didn't respond. He thought she looked kind of sick, though. When Adi started to tell him about the pins and needles pricking her eyes, I bet the guy just wanted to get her out of his car.

"Hey darlin', sorry, I've got to go now."

I think Adi got angry slowly. The way he was telling her to leave and take the cash. He was saying: You'll be here forever. And I'll be here tomorrow.

Adi could smell his cock in her sweat.

"Adi, right? I got to go now. You hear me, right? I've got to go home. I'll come back tomorrow. You give the best head. I'm coming back tomorrow for ya, alright?"

And I think she knew then: she was in a car, just down the street from the club, with the curse of a cock being laid back in pants, with a mouth full of spit and loathing and sperm. I bet Adi rose, whipped her head back, lipstick smeared on her yellow-white teeth and screamed: "Cocksucking mother-fucking father-fucking fuck! There's hairs on your asshole. There's veins in your shit! There's skin scratching off the root of your cock. I hate you! I'll kill you! You ugly fucking fuck!"

I bet Adi limped out of the car. She walked a few paces and crouched down in a corner near some garage door. She looked like a squirrel chewing its hands.

I bet the guy saw her there, too, but he pulled out of the lot and drove away. Because the guy thought Adi would just go back when she was ready.

He didn't see her stick a hose up herself and start huffing. He didn't see the spit running black down her lips. Adi stuck there, forever stuck running.

I took Gio's car. I drove in the same direction we had gone before. I wanted to see the same trees, the same lights, the same telephone poles. I wanted to see the same ditches by the side of the road and the same plants in the field the same height as me.

But the road wouldn't focus in front of my eyes. It was the middle of the night when before it had been day. I knew I should stop for just half an hour and rest. I didn't know if it was possible to hurt more than I already did. My hands were shaking, raw on the wheel. I'd just touched his mouth. I'd just walked away. I'd just felt his body under my body and now his face was becoming my face. Gio was someone who shut his mouth with the muscles of his cheeks. When he smiled, it happened behind his mouth.

Now I was crying because I'd thought that I was the one who was going to make him happy. That his happiness would happen because I was the one who laid with him. It was my heart that opened up to his heart. My legs that opened up to his cock. I was the one who disappeared, became light, not a person, not a woman, not a whore, but the heat of my insides moving through his. My body was a suction, millions of suctions. I thought there was no other girl in the world who could have him.

Gio had stopped the car in the middle of the road and it felt like that time with my father, when I couldn't get out of the car. How he screamed at me: "Mira get out of the car!" He used the same voice that he used with the dog. He was the man in the driveway yelling for my mother: "She won't get out of the car! She won't get out of the car!" My father's dull body with his face full of hair, hair around his lips and a voice full of spite. He was a person with skin red from yelling. That was what I knew inside the car, with my legs squeezed together, with my mother at the door, her head leaning in: "What's wrong with you Mira?"

My mother spoke to my father with hoarseness in her throat. She said: "Go in the house. Everything's fine."

My mother told my father I was fine.

With my mother's head poking back into the car, it was easy to get out.

"What is it, Mira?" She said something like that. "What is wrong with you?" Sighing. "I'm sure there's a reason."

My mother put her arm around me even though I felt too old for hugs. We walked slowly to the house. We walked slowly up the stairs. It was all too gloomy between my mother and me, when I should have laughed, I was on the verge of laughing...

Back in my room though, when I was fifteen, I knew for certain that something was wrong. It didn't even matter what that something was. I knew it because of the way my mother looked at me after she told my father that everything was fine. I knew that both of them believed now that something wasn't fine but neither of them knew exactly what it was. Or exactly how to talk to me ever again.

The problem with my father yelling and the problem with my mother's gloom was that the problem was mine. If some guy was looking at me on the street, if I was seeing men in my room, strange men at my back, the problem was mine. The problem was mine.

I knew right then that I'd have to slide like a snake from my home. If I wanted to breathe without tears in my throat, if I wanted to ever learn to explode, I'd have to hold in my gut and slither away. Because what your parents think about you is true. What your father thinks, what your mother thinks, all of it is perfectly true.

Your body is helpless so far from the ground. You're see-through and if you don't slide away, you'll stay and you'll lie and be filled up with poison.

When a girl's body is just starting to be formed, people teach her to ignore the men in the street. Just ignore and ignore and all will be fine. If there's a buzzing in your pants, don't say a word. Even if something cracks loudly in your head, some rotting fence about to fall over, don't say a word. Because everything's fine.

But sometimes some things need to be said!

All great whores become pure, Gio said.

I pulled over on the shoulder. My breathing was too fast. My palms were so sweaty they were slipping off the wheel. I just sat there, hyperventilating in the darkness. Beside me was a huge field of corn. When a car drove by in the opposite direction, the stalks flashed from yellow to black. They were slick and alive.

I turned the keys and got out of the car.

I had to use my hands to make a path through the stalks, even though they were all growing from organized holes. The stalks rose unevenly to just above my head. I was walking so slowly, I felt my knees crack. My head sunk down. I inhaled manure.

Suddenly, I heard rustling behind me to the left. I thought it was a mouse. I stopped, froze. I couldn't walk further but I didn't want to go back. I didn't want to sit and I didn't want to stand. Why couldn't I just be there, perfectly still? Why couldn't I stand without moving around?

I took off Gio's jacket and dropped it on the ground. I loosened my jeans around my waist.

I was trembling, swaying side to side. My hips were moving on top of my legs in tiny circles. I realized I had to move from side to side just to stand still. There was only balance between both my legs. I was so uncomfortable I tried to lean over and look at my feet, but I couldn't bend down to see them without seizing up. The backs of my legs were spasming in pain.

So I let my head hang. I let my arms hang. I realized that all I'd really done in the past year was dance at the club, dance in high heels.

My legs felt dead. I hung there for a minute at least. Almost all of my body had turned into static. I felt blood in my eyes. My head was getting closer to the ground. I started to get used to the hanging, this feeling of trying to feel through the numbness.

Then something happened. Between my head and the earth, I felt hot little beats. I wrapped my arms around my legs, hugged my chest to my thighs. It felt so good to have my stomach in a fold. My teeth were on my thighs. My whole body was spiraling in on itself.

Gio said that the first time he saw me dancing, he felt ashamed. He told me that because everyone was paying for this, it meant everyone was praying for this. He explained I was up there because of men's longings. We all wanted you to be our whore, Gio said. And he said he didn't know if I could handle that yet. He said he didn't know if I knew how to soothe a man, yet. How to let a "strange man" love me for release. Gio said that the other girls made light of what they did — grabbing onto men's cocks for a living and forgetting. Gio said I was different. You can take the weight of it, he said, like Mary of Egypt, the holiest of holies, who died in the desert a saint.

All great whores become pure, Gio said.

The stretch in my body was making me scream. I felt spaces in my body that had never been used. I bent my knees deeper and reached my hands to the ground, but I lost my balance and fell into the earth.

Shit! Damn this pain!

My whole body was shocked. Needles were stabbing every single cell. I tried to shake it off, but it wouldn't stop. I lay on my back and writhed around. My head touched a stalk, my feet slapped the ground.

I dragged my hands into place for the trick. What I used to do onstage — press up in an arch with my legs planted wide, my cunt on the pole. I thought if I did it, the needles would stop. I shot my eyes up through the husks to the sky. I curled my hips towards me, slowly rising. My hands, my back, I was bending backwards… Hanging hair, hanging head, my spine cracked in stages. It felt like two hands were holding under my ass, just waiting for the cracking to go up through my chest, up to where my heart was racing. From my tailbone to the highest part of my back, in this crackling field, I could feel it coming. I was the one who was making these cracks come!

Amen! Amen! Mother of God!

My head rolled over a leaf and a stone. Blacked out, tingling, my mouth had curled up. It was still going, my teeth were still ringing, my heart was still spasming… I hadn't danced at the club, I'd never danced! All I was doing was fucking the air!

Air surged through my toes to my scalp. My body felt opened. It was bigger than the sky.

God, there is so much to feel without starting in my ass!

When I finally stumbled back to the car, my knees were so weak, like the joints were gushing fluid. With my forehead on the wheel, I started to crack up. This crazy, crying laughter where the cracks just keep widening... God, I was coming apart and I didn't know where the parts were going!

Are you happy Gio? Do you feel like this?

Maybe Gio told me what I needed to hear. All of my life what I needed to hear: that we fuck and it's gone, that we fuck and it's in us. If a girl does not at some point become pure — from pure into dirt and from dirt back to gold — then nothing could truly happen in this world. We'd never come out from a mother and father. We'd never find people stroking us, needing... But sex was a hitch, sweat got me drunk. Things came through men's pores, through the creases in their necks. I left Gio there because I was afraid. Afraid of feelings jutting up inside me.

I didn't feel pure! I never felt pure!

I want my body to feel the way I feel now. I want it to move in the air above streams going over the rocks, going endlessly more...

Gio made me feel that nothing changes. Nothing weakens, nothing splits. And if we went back to his house, I would feel the same things, because he would be him and I would be me and we would be us... It's all so addictive. Nothing changes. Coming back to him with mud in my hair, come on my thighs and he'd tell me that Jesus does not desire the death of sinners. We must bring forth what is inside us or else it will destory us... I just want this feeling of endlessness one more time! As small as a pebble or huge as a bull, I just need this feeling to push on my navel. One more time!

Gio is the birth of this feeling in me. That's why he's my real mother. Why I am all his...

Gio told me God loved me because I was strong enough for this. He said the whore is the only one strong enough to receive the wrath of men. The charge between man and whore is so strong. Men cannot just turn around when she is in their path.

"We all know when we're with a whore that nothing will ever be perfectly right. The scum of the world will always rest on the periphery…

"You and I both see this," Gio said. "Like blotches at the sides of our eyes."

The rest stop shone up ahead like a city.

I ran into the bathroom, went straight to a stall and checked my underwear: there was barely any more blood. When I came out and saw myself in the mirror, I laughed — my hair was clumped on top of my head in a nest. I looked like some animal fresh from the woods with no one there to lick her clean.

A woman walked into the bathroom. I started splashing water on my face so it didn't look like I'd just been talking to myself. I tried to comb the knots out of my hair with my fingers but it didn't work. The woman was making noises in the toilet stall, straining high-pitched whines like a child trying to go to the bathroom. I put some lipstick on and went out to the payphone.

I paced in front of the phone. I thought maybe I should get some coffee first. I wasn't even sure I remembered his number.

There were just a few people eating in the main room. The guy who served me coffee didn't look at my face. I asked him how far we were from the city. He told me it was about a twenty-minute drive. I thought I'd been driving and in that field for at least an hour.

I took my coffee to a table and stared up at the ceiling. Fake painted logs met together in a triangle. Soft rock played from speakers hanging under a big clock. It was four in the morning. I realized that the woman from the washroom was sitting one table over from me. She was by herself, chin sunk in her hand. She looked like a mother. Her cheeks and eyes sagged. I assumed that she was waiting for her husband who was in the bathroom. She caught me looking at her and smiled, an open-lipped smile that showed all the wrinkles in her face.

The woman pointed at me. "Alone?"

I smiled.

"Why're you alone?"

She got up and walked sluggishly over to my table. Her pants were strangely loose around her hips. Her black hair was frizzy, even the bangs.

"I don't know, no reason," I said.

She sat down too close to me and cradled her face. Her breasts were huge. She smelled like sickly sweet red wine.

"Good to be alone at night, I come here alone in the car. I learned to drive, just been two years. It's good to drive alone at night, just like you. You coming from where?"

"From the city."

I wanted to spin my chair away from the table, but I knew it would be rude. She was breathing on my mouth, looking at me almost lovingly.

"Used to live there too," she said, nodding her head slowly. "Was an okay place when I lived there, not like now. Too many problems in the city now. When I lived there it was nice. You at school?"

"No. Work."

"Help people, yes?"

"I guess."

"Very smart thing to be helping other people."

That made me laugh.

"I try to help people, too — don't laugh — since my husband and me came here and never looked back…"

The woman's eyes glazed over. Her chin dipped suddenly off her palm.

"Ha! I want to see more and he doesn't want to see a thing. I wanted to see more in my life than just home and come here, home and come here. I could've done more with myself than just home and come here, home and come here. I want to see things. See the things. People on buildings, those barefoot ones who live above the ceilings, who are fixing the roof so the rain doesn't kill them. I want to see them, but Ali's got sick and I sit home and it's fine to take care of him, fine. He's the same one who promised my father he wouldn't let me live like a monkey on a roof. My father was an architect. It's true. Don't believe me?"

The woman stared at my hands as she talked. "You know the people in houses who live around us can see us? Us doing our business from behind… I never have a moment to walk out the way I used to. My breasts are on my stomach, you see? I used to be a good-looking girl, believe me. People said I was a beauty. Don't believe me? When Ali sees me before I go to bed and he's doing his business, he always has time to yell at me, 'Dina, your body is bigger than mine!' I don't even tell him it was always bigger, I was always bigger than him. Now in the bed I come back to his diapers, his thing, and the last thing he does in this world is yell and yell, no talking, all yelling."

Dina suddenly looked up at the huge clock on the wall.

"You see? I have to get back now. He's up in fifteen minutes for the pills."

The chair made a screech as she got up. I raised my hand. She looked over her shoulder to say goodbye. I watched her walk out the door and fall into her car. She sat there unmoving behind the thick windshield. I couldn't see her eyes but I still thought she was watching me.

The guy who'd served me coffee came up beside me. "That old bitch is always here," he said, laughing. "Don't worry about her."

"I'm not worried," I said.

"So what'chyou doing then?"

"Fuck off."

I got up and walked out of the restaurant.

In the parking lot, trucks were breathing noisily. I'd forgotten where I'd parked Gio's car. A horn beeped at me twice.

"Sssst. Here. Over here!"

Dina was leaning her head out of her car, her split black hair hanging down to the handle. She beeped again.

"Hey! Come over here for a second! Sssst!"

I walked up to her slowly. It was as if her head was disconnected from her shoulders.

"Okay," she slurred. "Okay, I won't drive. You'll drive? Yes? I need to get back to him. Red pills in five. Drive me to the lights. I didn't know tonight. You were here. I was okay."

Dina cranked her neck up at me, she was hiccuping.

"He's calling, Din-Din-Dina! Din-Din-Dina! Just two seconds away, I hear Din-Din-Dina!"

She somehow lifted up her head from the car door, unlocked it and slid over to the passenger's side. The door swung open. The keys were in the ignition. Dina gave me a sloppy smile as I sat down in the driver's seat. The car smelled like wine. She was giggling.

"Thank you, thank you, little Din-Din-Dina!"

I pulled out of the parking lot and onto a small road behind the rest stop. There were no other cars. We were in a safe void. Dina kept saying home wasn't too far. She pointed directions for me until we were in some kind of suburban area where the houses were built with sloping roofs and all the driveways curved so you could drive right up to the front door.

"Here!" Dina shouted.

I stopped and pulled into the driveway of the darkened house. It was lit up by a lamp stuck in the grass. Dina fumbled to take the keys out of the ignition.

"Come in," she said. "With Dina. Drive you back in two-four seconds."

It was as if she were suddenly even more drunk. Dina jogged clumsily to the front door. She looked back at me with her finger motioning in front of her lips. She had some kind of conspiratorial smile on her face.

When I got to the front door, she whispered: "You hear?"

Inside the house it was way too warm. Dina turned on a light. A huge chandelier lit up carpeted stairs.

"Here, pee-pee, here…" Dina cooed.

A brown and black-spotted cat ran in from the hallway. It leapt up into Dina's arms. She held it close to her mouth and started making purring noises.

I did hear something. A weak beat from upstairs.

Din-din-din… Din-din-din…

I looked up the staircase and then over at Dina. Her eyes were drooping down towards her cat. She was starting to look familiar. The place stunk of wine.

"I've got to get going," I said softly.

Dina kept purring. "No, no wait, pee-pee. I'll be back in a second. You see how he needs me?"

Dina made it to the stairs. She looked strangely regal with the tail of the cat curled around her waist. Step after step, then she disappeared.

I knew I wouldn't be able to walk back to the rest stop by myself, so I just stood there waiting. I counted the lines in the wallpaper: thick gold stripes beside thin olive bands. I counted the stairs. I counted the tiles on the floor. I didn't want to wait.

I walked into the living room. Two long couches were lined up right beside each other and there was a lamp hanging low from a chain in the corner. The room was lit up by streetlight. I walked up to the bookshelf. It sounded like crickets. Between some of the books were these antique-looking clocks.

I closed my eyes and listened to the shelves ticking. I could stand better now. My spine felt straight. I reached my arms up and felt for a book. I picked one and kept my eyes closed to the couch. *The Spirits' Book* by Allen Kardec.

What was it with me and this stuff? The cover had a picture of a man coloured yellow with a full moon rising above his head. A thin open hand was reaching in from the left side to help him.

I split the book in half and squinted to read: "Why does God permit spirits to incite us to evil?"

Yeah, tell me Kardec, why is it God's fault I'm evil?

"Imperfect spirits are used by Providence as instruments for tying men's faith and constancy in well-doing. You, being a spirit, must advance in the knowledge of the infinite."

Amen!

"It is for this end," the book continued, "that you are made to pass through the trials of evil in order to maintain goodness. Our mission is to lead you to the right road."

Well at least everyone is saying the same thing...

"When you are acted upon by evil influences, it is because you attract evil spirits to you with your evil desires, for evil spirits always come to aid you in doing the evil you desire to do; they can only help you do wrong when you give way to evil desires. If you are inclined to commit murder, you will have about you a swarm of spirits who will keep this inclination alive in you, but you will also have others about you who will try to influence you for good, which restores the balance, and leaves you of your decision."

So does evil always come before good?

All of a sudden I remembered the strange men who came to my room, men who watched me through the darkness when I was a girl. Men who stood over my bed while I pretended to sleep. There was this one night, when everything changed. Because one of those men spoke to me out loud. The strange men had always spoken in my head, so the second this one spoke in the air, all of the others were instantly gone. The man was loud enough that I thought my parents would come running up from downstairs. He leaned over my bed, swaying back and forth, and he sang in a language I didn't fully understand. Gibberish, slurring, with his hands clasped together, with my hands between my legs, a low, scratching song:

> *Girl like you, a girl like you.*
> *Off your bed and on your knees.*
> *Girl like you, a girl like you.*

I realized then, in the black and blue dark that this man wanted me to touch him back.

I couldn't touch him, though. I wouldn't reach my arms out. So he just kept singing:

> *Get off your bed.*
> *Get on your knees.*
> *Get off your bed.*
> *Get on your knees.*

I pulled the covers up to my ears. I was afraid of his voice. This strange man had come before I knew what to do. I plugged my ears. I squeezed my eyes. I shook my head from side to side: "Go away! Go away! Go away! Go away!"

And the strange man disappeared with a high yelping cry. A cry so loud that I knew my parents would come up this time. But they didn't come. I told myself it meant the man wouldn't come back for me either.

Wait, was it true what this book was saying? Have strange men, spirits, been following me around? Is this why I picked *The Spirits' Book* off the shelf? Could spirits enter people's heads just like I'd walked into this house? Could spirits make me do things? Could spirits make me fuck?

I met that strange man during my childhood night and sparks flew from his mouth in front of my face... And I knew that someone existed. There was something else in the world, something real but invisible to others, someone who needed something only from me.

"Ssssst! Here, here!"

I slammed the book shut. Dina was whistling. I quickly went out to the entranceway. Dina was there, at the top of the stairs, wearing a skirt, with her hair combed back. She looked completely different. Her face was all flushed.

"You waited, good."

Dina walked down the stairs. Her legs were nicer than the rest of her body. She smiled. "He's sleeping now. Let's take you back."

She had put on perfume. I smelled vanilla when she opened the door. I was outside and already standing at the car when I looked up and saw that she hadn't even left the doorway. Dina was framed by the golden stripes of the wallpaper.

"Will you come back in for a second?" she asked sweetly, tilting her head to one side. "Will you come up with me, help me for a second?"

I don't know what happened while I was watching her. It was like she was someone from my family, like I knew her...

I found myself walking up to the door. I followed Dina up the stairs. I touched the wallpaper, over the stripes. I smelled the weird milky smell of some child long gone.

"Here. He's in here."

A man was lying still with the sheets up to his neck in a room with dusty light-pink walls. His eyes were open but he wasn't seeing. His hair was so dead it was yellow.

"Ali, this is…"

Dina looked at me.

"Mira," I said.

"Mira. A beautiful girl named Mira has come to visit."

I thought I saw Ali's fingers move under the sheet. Dina walked kind of seductively up to her husband. She sat down at the edge of his bed and put her hand on the sheet where his stomach was. "This young lady was nice enough to come up here and help me, so I want you to be good, okay?"

Ali didn't move. He closed his eyes. Slowly, Dina started to peel the sheets from his body. Five single sheets on top of a man. I walked closer. I knew this was a man who hadn't spoken for a while, or he was a man who'd been struck dumb by speaking.

What was he about to say?

Shiny eye. Pretty girl. Suck her puss. Love my wife.

The man was immobile. His nose was a beak.

What was he about to say?

We have all committed crimes that have cursed us.

Dina had rolled down almost all the sheets. They were carefully folded at Ali's knees. One sheet was left, covering his body like tissue paper. Dina looked at her husband and then up at me.

"Here here here it is…"

Underneath the sheet, God, his skin was littered with marks — shining red circles, even brighter at the edges. You couldn't see nipples. Because everything, everywhere, was bright red protrusions.

"You see?" Dina smiled. "This is the one I live with. You see how they used to say I'm a looker?"

I put my hand over my mouth as Dina leaned down to kiss her husband's chest. Strained little cries escaped someone's lips. Dina pulled down the rest of the sheet and with her free hand exposed the man's penis. It was bright white and hairless, standing halfway erect. His dick was the only clear thing on him.

"He would like it, look."

Ali hadn't made a sound. His eyes were closed, eyeballs roaming under the lids. It was like he existed somewhere over his body, or both of them were moving without leaving their skin. With Ali hovering and Dina's curved arms, I saw them together in a big figure eight.

Dina gestured towards Ali's penis. She spit on her hand and grabbed him really quick. Moving up and down and up and down, I'd never seen such a fast job without oil. Dina was still kissing his chest.

It looked like some kind of painting to me: the two of them lying there, fixed and cracked. I thought that this was something I'd seen before, something I'd even been in front of before, with my hands held out, held out to help. I was leaning towards them…

"Yes," Dina murmured.

My hand reached down to touch Ali's cock. It was satiny and my fingers formed into a fist. I started moving my hand on top of Dina's. It moved exactly like hers, bouncing at the same speed.

Then she let me do it alone. I was looking out over the wreck of Ali's chest while Dina started kissing, then fondling his balls. I think she put a finger inside his ass. Ali was moaning. I was going to pass out. I was fighting it off. I knew I could do it longer, help her like this…

"Mira, he's coming. Ali, you're coming."

I felt her tongue licking. I heard myself grunting like I was the one coming. Like I was the man shooting up towards the sky!

"Good good good…"

Creamy white stuff came out on my fingers. Ali was staring at us with dazzling eyes. Gold and black eyes, the eyes of a swan.

Dina handed me a cloth from the side of the bed.

"Wipe yourself off," she said happily. "Let's take you home. Ali, Mira was good! The way you like."

Ali opened his mouth wide. Nothing came out. But I heard deep humming from him somewhere in the room.

Back in the car, Dina was giggling and sighing. "My stupid little fool," she gushed.

The sky was starting to lose its blackness.

"It's good we were in love, that makes it better," said Dina. She was driving clumsily out of the driveway. The clock shone green: 5:13. "It's something only a woman knows, what happens to a man when he's looking at his wife who's been wiping his body every day for years. You cut off his head and he still has his thing, the thingy he used to use."

"He still wants to be with you," I said. The humming from his throat was still in my head.

"No, no," Dina laughed. She took a flask out of the glove compartment and had a quick swig. "I do it like he used to. I took over from him."

"No, I mean you can see that he really loves you."

Dina drove me back the rest of the way in silence. A blurred line of sky ended at the parking lot. Dina pulled in and drove me right up to the entrance of the restaurant. She'd already had five or six big gulps of booze.

"Thanks to my little assistant," she said.

I got out of the car, slamming the door too hard. I looked back through the window at Dina's peering, blinking eyes. A vertical crease was starting to form between her eyebrows. She was smiling at me widely as the gouge deepened. Her frizzy hair formed a halo around her face. Before I could say anything, she drove away.

I was cradling the phone.

"Ezrah?"

Silence.

"Hey, Ezrah?"

Silence.

"It's me, Mira."

I heard a soft cough.

"Hey Ezrah, come on. It's early, I know…"

"What do you want?" It sounded like his mouth was full. "Why are you calling me in the middle of the night?"

I took the phone away from my cheek.

"Wait," Ezrah said, swallowing constantly. "Wait, it's just late, alright?"

"No, you're right. I shouldn't have called right now…"

"Where are you?"

"Not sure."

"What the fuck do you mean you're not sure? No one's heard from you in months. My mom said your mom hasn't heard from you ın months! They don't even have a phone number for you, Mira. Your mom's mad. At first she was worried, but now she's just mad. I don't even know if she's going to talk to you when you call. You're gonna call her right? Do it now. You have to call her."

"I called you, Ezrah. I don't want to talk to my mother right now."

"Fuck! They just keep asking me if I've talked to you. I say, yeah I have and you're doing fine, you just don't feel like talking right now. But I can't do that anymore. It's been months, for fuck's sake! Some girl died around there. Did you know that Mira? I was freaking out and I couldn't tell anyone, you hear me? I was freaking out. They found a girl's body half an hour from you, she was completely naked, they knew she was a sex worker. Whatever, that's what they called her in the papers…"

"I haven't read the papers."

"I went down to the fucking police station, I drove all the way to the morgue with some cop to see this poor girl. You know why I did that, huh?"

I knew.

"Because I thought it was you. Because I thought it was you. Because I fucking thought it was you!"

"I'm sorry…"

"No. The cops told me they found saliva in her, not semen, just saliva. They don't even think she's from here, they think she's from Russia somewhere, or Poland somewhere. No one's come to get her. No one knows anything about her. All the girls at your club are Russian or something, aren't they? It's disgusting. She was so skinny. Her face was black around the eyes. Some asshole beat her up and her nose was all fucked up. She looked like a crow. I was the only fucking one who'd come down to see her! The police took a swab from my mouth, they said we know it's not you, but no one's come to get her. No one!"

I steadied my breath.

"Did you know her? Mira?"

"Yes."

I closed my eyes and this is what I saw: on an empty highway with marked-up poles and drooping-down wires, Adi's head at the side of the road. It was stuck in the gravel, neck trimmed, no gore. I crouched down close. I wasn't afraid. Because I saw there were words etched into her forehead. Green and black letters that had bled through the skin.

It was written: *This one lived according to my wishes.*

"She's okay," I whispered, wanting to throw up. My mouth felt full, full of white cud.

"I want to come get you. It doesn't matter where you are. I'll drive and come get you. Where are you, Mir? Just tell me."

Ezrah's voice had changed for a moment. But still I couldn't tell him where or how I was. I pressed my forehead into the receiver.

"How's school?" I asked.

"Why are you asking me that now? What's going on?"

"Just tell me how you are. That's why I called."

"No, for fuck's sake. Tell me where you are!"

"I left, okay? That's it. That's all."

"Oh God. Thank God."

Ezrah was excited. Why was he so excited?

"God, Mir, that's good. That's amazing. I'm so relieved. That's amazing."

"Okay."

"I'm so happy, Mira. That stuff wasn't for you. You know that now, don't you?"

What I know is that you are exactly the same.

"Hey, Mir?"

"What."

""Why don't you come stay with me down here for a while? I don't have my exams until December. I'm just here, studying, whatever. We can hang out for a few weeks. Or you can stay longer, it doesn't matter. Why don't you come down here and stay with me? My room's alright, it's big enough…"

"I'm just calling to say hi, Ezrah."

"I want us to hang out again."

"Why?"

"Come on, don't do this…"

"No, tell me why."

""I don't know, because I want you to be happy..."

"I am happy."

"Come on, that's not true! Your voice sounds all weird."

The cud in my mouth now was lining the walls.

"Mira, I thought you were dead. Do you actually understand that?"

I was about to hang up.

"Wait, Mir, just wait where you are. I'm going to come get you. Just stay where you are and I'm going to come right over there and get you."

I held the phone far away from my face.

"Don't go yet, Mira!"

"Why?"

"Because I miss you. I mean, I really, really miss you."

The phone cord was wrapped three times around my wrist.

"Mira?"

"Look, Ezrah, I'll see you soon, I just think I should be alone right now…"

"No, you shouldn't! Why haven't you called me all this time?"

"Come on, you know why."

"No, I don't."

"I didn't want to talk to you."

"Don't say that. I don't want to hear you saying that."

Now I was the one starting to get mad.

"Fuck it, Ezrah! How can you forget?"

"Forget what?"

"You were disgusted."

"No…"

"You were."

"I was not…"

"Yes, you were. You still are. In fact you've always been kind of disgusted with me."

"Look, Mira, I just couldn't be okay with all that… You in that place, all those guys, doing that… I'm sorry. Sorry, okay? I couldn't help it. It just wasn't for me. Come on, I think most people would understand that."

But love comes from disgust. Trusting disgust.

"Mira? I said I'm sorry. Don't you understand? Fuck, I thought you were dead…"

"I get it."

"It's just that I know you can do something better with your life, that's it. That's all. Believe me."

"Yeah."

"Talk to me. Just keep talking to me, okay?"

"Okay."

"Mira?"

"Okay, I'll keep talking."

Silence.

"Please."

"Okay. That girl you saw dead? Well she was in love. And the guy she was in love with? Well he was the one who told me what I was doing there, what men were doing with me…"

"What are you talking about?"

"Being there. Me being at the club."

"Okay…"

"It made sense."

"What made sense?"

"It's hard to explain…"

"Try."

"Okay. Just wait."

I took a deep breath. Flashing quickly through my head: Adi the Warrior, Ali the Swan.

"There's this story in the Bible about Hosea, he's a prophet…"

"Yeah. I know that story."

"Okay, so Hosea marries a whore because God tells him to, because God wants to show him the meaning of love, because God will always love the whore."

"The whore? Mira, who is this guy?"

"A guy, a friend who came to the place."

"What, some guy you danced for?"

"No."

"You're lying."

"No, I'm not."

"Yes, you are. What? Was he your boyfriend, too? You fucked that dead girl's boyfriend?"

"Shut up!"

Silence numbed the line again.

"I shouldn't have called."

"Fuck it, Mira, just go on. What about Hosea and his whore?"

"I shouldn't have called you."

"You're frustrating me."

"Yeah?"

"Look, I want to understand, but you're frustrating me. Let me come and get you now, that's all I want to do. Okay?"

"It's not a good idea."

""Fuck!"

"I should be telling someone else. I should be telling everyone else."

"What? Telling them what?"

"That Hosea loves his whore, no matter what she's done."

I heard Ezrah's breathing slow right down. I kept talking into the sudden space.

"I'm saying there are these moments when you can be ready to die, moments when your strength, your whole life starts to fade. The light goes down just an inch from your eyes and you think your whole life was lived up to this moment and your vision is perfect from one end of the world to the other..."

"Okay, Mira..."

"No, no, Ezrah, wait. I've felt all these things from what I've been doing. I mean it was a whole other world in that place, in that club, everyone had different weight to their feet, everyone was heavier and we were all attached to each other too much. If someone was slimy, I had the same slime. It wasn't the law of opposites attract: the girls were like the girls and the slime was like the slime. It's good to be a pig rolling in the slime sometimes, Ezrah... Because now I know what everyone pays for, now I know whose body pays more. I've been there trying to clean it all up. Or clean up the layers and squeeze it out in tubes. I have been trying to organize people's unbearable needs because I see their unbearable forms. A triangle up is not the same thing as a triangle down. But a tube up and a tube down is exactly the same thing. All I want is for things to be equal."

Ezrah was about to protest...

"All the feelings I had there have rebounded and hit me in the chest. Shame was just everything that hit me in the chest before the feeling came full circle."

"I don't understand," Ezrah said slowly.

"I had these moments in the dark in that crappy little room when I could literally see from the back of my head…"

"Stop, Mira, please…"

"And there was this gluey white thread there, floating in the air, it was about halfway between the bed and the ceiling. I knew that this cord had been whipped around the earth…"

I heard Ezrah snort back to life, a nervous reaction in his nose.

"I want to wait for more of this, Ezrah, I want to wait every night, ruined or not. It feels good seeing these kind of things, like your brain's practically dripping from the walls, like your brain can act outside your head, moving without static…" My voice suddenly got hoarse. "Will you tell my mom that I called?" I heard myself asking. "Tell her I'm okay. Tell her I'll call her."

"No."

"Please, Ezrah. Just tell her I'll call her. Tell her I love her. I've got to go now."

"I'm coming there. I'm going there right now. I'm going exactly where I went for you last time and I'm going in the back door and I'm going up to your shitty little room on that shitty second floor. I don't care who's in there, I'm going to pound his face in. You happy now, Mira? I bet you're there anyway. I bet you never left that fucking shit hole."

"Don't you dare go there. I am not there."

"I don't believe you. I'm going. Getting my shoes on. Getting my car keys…"

"Ezrah, I mean it. Don't go."

"I'm leaving in two minutes, coming to get you. It'll take me a half hour. See you."

"Don't!"

"What? Is your boyfriend sleeping there? Is that it? I'll pound his face in if he's there."

"Ezrah, fuck!"

"Ezrah fuck what?"

It was the last thing I heard. My fingers were bright red. I ran out of the rest stop and down the road. Back.

They were waiting for me on opposite sides of the room.

Gio on the edge of my bed and Ezrah in darkness, arms crossed at the wall. I turned on the light and walked quickly past Ezrah, to Gio, who reached out his arm like a branch.

"Who's this?" he asked.

"He hates me!" I shouted.

I was completely freaked out from driving so fast, from running up the stairs and turning on the lights. I'd raced here to stop this: Gio and Ezrah. I wasn't ready to go through this end.

"You have to tell him to leave then, Mira."

Red patches rose up and flushed Ezrah's face. "Just fuck off man, okay?"

My bottom lip started to shake in spasms.

"You're coming home with me, Mira. Just come now, okay?"

I couldn't hold anything in anymore. My throat filled up, my eyes started to itch. Right in this hole, in front of Gio, in front of Ezrah, I scratched and rubbed nervously, about to shit…

"It's okay," Ezrah whispered. "I wanted to see you alone. That's all."

He was walking right towards me. I had to move away.

"But I'm different now, Ezrah. I'm different, you see?""

"I don't care Mira, please…"

God, what is this place that it can break people's hearts? This place where men come to fuck their own daughters. This maze where fathers and daughters meet up...

"Excuse me," Gio said. "I think I can explain. Nothing is wrong here. What has taken place here isn't wrong."

"Wait," I warned, without looking behind me.

A grotesque looking smile loosened Ezrah's face. He already thought I was coming with him? I wanted to say: just hang on there, you…

I heard some of the girls whispering outside my door. I knew they'd probably seen who was here. Her family come to save her! Big brother's come to take her! My hand was touching the side of my head. It felt numb at my temple, like rock touching rock.

All I wanted was to be back in the field, with the thousands of stalks growing twisted from holes. I wanted my nerves to flap green in the sun.

"I think I can explain this," Gio said.

"Wait!" I screamed and whipped around. Gio's black eyes narrowed in on me tightly.

"Mira has come here and come back here of her own accord," Gio said to Ezrah as he reached for my wrist. "If you want to see her, you'll have to stay here."

My free arm was dangling hot.

"Why doesn't she tell me to leave then, you asshole? Mir? Why don't you tell me to leave? Just tell me to go and I'll go, okay?"

If I could have, I would have stayed there longer, stuck in between them, heat and direction…

"But it's not you who has to go, it's Mira who has to stay," Gio repeated. "She still has work to do tonight."

Gio squeezed my wrist in tightening pulses.

"You don't know what the fuck you're saying," Ezrah shouted. "She's my family and she can do what she wants!"

"Why don't you come over here then, mmm? To your family."

"I'm not going to do what you fucking tell me! Mira, Jesus, who is this guy?"

"Why don't you come over here to Mira's feet."

"Fuck off, do you hear me? Why don't you fucking leave us alone?"

I knew I had to say something soon. Nothing either of them was saying was true. I pleaded silently with Gio to stop now, stop, but it didn't work, my head was too thick. So I couldn't do a thing as he kneeled down before me, as he took off my shoes and started cradling my feet.

"The ground is the place we begin with the whore," Gio said, looking up at Ezrah. "We weep and then we make our supplication."

The skin on his cheeks was beating and hard. Gio smiled at me before he set his lips down. He kissed me in sequence, starting with my big toes. His mouth slid quickly down the line and he lingered forever on my last little toe. I felt my feet stretch out to reach his chin. Heat rained down on his head from my thighs.

"I'm not into the shit you guys are into here," Ezrah said nervously as he watched us.

I had power over the room. I was watching the room repent.

Gio motioned to Ezrah from the ground.

"No, fuck off. That's not for me. It's disgusting you just let him do that, Mira."

My whole body was pounding. I felt ready to explode. Why are some people happy to linger in things while some people need to rush anxiously through?

Ezrah was moving towards the door. His face was a wreck.

"Ezrah, I want you to stay."

He stopped, frigid, and stared at my toes.

"I want you to. I'm sorry. Don't leave us right now, okay?"

I watched Ezrah falter. I thought he was going to faint. But he started shuffling in tiny steps towards us. Gio immediately got up and sat on the edge of the bed. I knew me and him both saw the same thing — Ezrah lumbering, half-hearted, falling down to his knees. We were bringing him into a space that everyone could feel.

The top of Ezrah's head bobbed lightly up and down. His mouth was barely touching my feet. His thick brown hair hid the motion of his jaw. My feet were the wood. His saliva was dew. I made noises like sex. Wetness was cruelty.

"I can't do this," Ezrah said, grabbing onto my ankles.

My feet got cold without the feeling of his breath. I felt a smile in my face that didn't get stuck.

"Keep going, you can," Gio said gently, looking at me. "You were doing it, go. Put your mouth back, she loves it, she loves what you're doing, she's going to come, you're making her come. Go on, keep going, your mouth on her body is making her come."

"Don't stop," I said, echoing Gio.

Ezrah licked his lips and looked up at me from the ground. The whites of his eyes were gleaming out of the sea. I imagined them pierced by the beaks of huge golden birds. I revealed more to Ezrah by showing my teeth. We would never look at each other exactly like this again.

"I love you," I mouthed. The room felt so bright.

Ezrah understood my new smile. His head dropped to my feet. He kissed each toe wet. He was better this time. I couldn't keep my eyes off him.

"She's touching herself. She's rubbing herself, keep doing what you're doing, she's going to come. Faster, come on, faster. She's doing it for you. You're making her come. Go on, come too, yeah, take it out, rub your cock, that's good, you're making her come, make yourself come, you're making her come..."

I watched Ezrah rubbing from way up above. The friction of his fist and the feeling of his tongue, my feet flared through my heart to my head. Pulsing because. And pulsing because. Wet steady pressure and realms opened up, men opened up, holes opened up. "Oh God! God, yeah!"

My head jerked back. I let go. I gave way.

"Mira, Mira…"

Juice shot down my thighs and reached Ezrah's face.

"Your life will be saved like a bitch from the noose."

"Mira, Mira..."

My name up and down was a double-headed bird.

"Mira, Mira…"

With my eyes squeezed shut, I felt a hot burn. Flickering stripes hit the base of my skull. I didn't know who was saying my name. My head rolled to the left and I opened my eyes.

Where did you go? Gio, God.

My head rolled to the right and I felt a hot tear. Droplets of salt in the corner of my mouth.

"Thank God we're gone, thank God we're gone."

Ezrah was pulling me by the arm, through doors, into hallways, into dark, almost day. I felt nauseous one second, floating the next. I slid into his car with the soft leather seats. He started it up before I'd even shut the door.

"Wait!" I said, like I always said: "Wait!"

We were whipping through the empty streets. I watched us pass all the houses with flat and locked doors. Ezrah was anxious and serious. He thought he was taking me away.

Gio? You see? He's taking me away.

I looked over at Ezrah, but he kept his eyes on the road. I reached out and rubbed down the creases in his sweater.

"Don't worry right now, Ezrah. Okay?"

The warm and clean space of his car had relaxed me. I looked out my window and leaned my head against the glass. There was nothing to see but the light and its rising. This brightest of lights that scatters all nights, that surrounds and reveals every object for morning. Morning isn't broken. It comes in relieved.

Reference is made to the following authors and works:

Kathy Acker, *In Memorium to Identity*. Pantheon Books, 1990 "Why do women become whores?" ❧ Friedrich Nietzsche, *Thus Spoke Zarathustra*, Fourth Part, 19. The Portable Nietzsche, The Viking Press, 1968 "In happiness too there are heavy animals…" ❧ The Baal Shem Tov, *Tales of the Hasidim, Early Masters*. Martin Buber, Schocken Books, 1975 "Truth is driven out of one place after another…" ❧ The Life of Saint Mary of Egypt as told by Sophronious, *Medieval Saints, A Reader*. Ed. Mary-Ann Stouck, Broadview Press, 1999 "I am nourished now by incorruptible food…"

The devotional love songs written by princess Mirabai to her beloved god Krishna are translated by Andrew Schelling in *For Love of The Dark One*, Shambhala Centaur Editions, 1993. "In a dream/the Lord of the Downtrodden/married Mira and took her to bed — /good fortune from previous births/bears its fruit."

This book is dedicated with love to Clement.

SUSAN WINEMAKER

Tamara Faith Berger lives in Toronto, Canada.